STILL GOT IT

A SPICY LATER IN LIFE ROMANCE SERIES

STILLWATER SPRINGS
BOOK TWO

JEM JOHNSON

THOSE JOHNSON GIRLS

Cover Design by Ines Johnson
Edited by Kasi Alexander

FOREWORD

TRIGGER WARNING

This isn't a typical trigger warning because there isn't much behavior in this book that would make most uncomfortable. That is unless you work in the field of law.

I take some liberties with legal ethics in this book. And you might get annoyed if you work in this arena. So I'm warning you upfront. Laws are not broken by the hero and heroine, but ethical lines are walked right up to and maybe even smudged, depending on your viewpoint.

I was warned by my legalese friends.

I chose to ignore some of their warnings in favor of a fun story.

Again, you have been warned.

Just remember that this is fiction, and I have no license to practice anything except for operating a motor vehicle. And in that I have been ticketed before.

I've been told I have a resting cross-examination face.

It's not intentional. Years of motherhood and litigation will do that to a woman. You spend enough time arguing with judges, juries, and three daughters who think their excuses are airtight, and suddenly your face settles into a permanent expression of "Objection!"

The boy across the table shifted under my stare. He called himself Micky. His profile said forty-two. His face said twenty-eight. Twenty-nine if he moisturized.

"You said you graduated high school in '89?" I stirred my drink like it was a gavel waiting for the opportunity to smash the glass tumbler. "Big year. Tell me, who was your favorite New Kid on the Block?"

Micky's smile flickered, making him look like a confused little mouse. "Oh, I wasn't into boy bands."

"More of a Skid Row kinda guy?"

His brows creased as though he was trying to place the metal band. Or maybe piece together those two words.

"Twisted Sister?"

"Oh, I did like girl bands."

I was so down with sustaining this guy and his obvious perjury. But I didn't correct him. No point. Cross-examinations work better when you let the witness dig their own grave.

"I see." I leaned in, tilting my head. "Where were you when the Berlin Wall fell?"

Micky's eyes darted left. "Remind me again… was that the, uh, political scandal thing?"

"That would be Watergate. Which, for the record, happened before you were even a twinkle in anyone's eye."

He laughed nervously, glancing at his beer mug like it might rescue him. "Look, I mean, history's not really my thing."

"Neither is honesty, apparently."

There it was. The flinch. They always flinched when you called it out plain.

This wasn't my first rodeo. Or my first cub.

Cougaring. That's what the kids called it these days. Some cute, predatory nickname they slapped on women my age so they could feel special about aiming low. Twenty-something boys looking for a "hot older woman" who'd stroke their egos, foot their dinner bill, and—if they played their cards right—teach them how to separate colors in the laundry.

I didn't come here to play teacher. I didn't come here to raise another man's sense of self. I came because I wanted my bean diddled after a hard day's work. A quick Tinder hookup was my kinda happy hour.

Micky wasn't even the worst of them. He was just the latest. Another kid who thought a few crow's feet made me a charity case. Charity in the bedroom but not in the bank.

The waiter slid two leather-bound menus onto the table and gave a polite nod. Micky picked his up like it was a quiz he hadn't studied for. I didn't bother. I already knew what I was getting. And that would be rid of my date.

He flipped through the pages, his brow furrowing. Then his lips pressed together. There were no prices printed on the paper. Micky placed the menu down on the table. Good boy. If you have to ask, you can't afford…

He looked up, blinking. "Sorry, what?"

"I said you're covering the check tonight, right? I mean, we're not doing that thing the kids do today and go Dutch or take turns paying for the meal. You're a real man of my generation. A gentleman like you doesn't believe in any of that crap."

Micky's throat worked like he was trying to swallow a boulder. He glanced back at the menu, as if prices might magically appear if he stared hard enough. They wouldn't. That's one of the reasons why I chose this particular bar.

"I… thought you were a feminist," Micky said, voice thin.

"Oh, I am. I'm also a grown-ass woman."

He looked around then, a quick, jittery scan of the restaurant, like he was mapping out exits. Front door, back door, maybe a window if things got desperate.

"You said you're a contractor." I kept my tone pleasant. Casual. Like I wasn't mentally pulling up the receipts.

"Yeah, I do a lot of freelance gigs."

"That's an interesting word for Uber driver."

His smile wobbled. Not enough to confess but enough to amuse me. "I hustle, you know? Gotta keep up with the cost of living these days."

"You know, when I was younger, we didn't have dating apps. We had bars, mutual friends, and the occasional Xeroxed flyer for a singles' mixer at the community center."

"Yeah, old-school dating, right? I love vintage vibes."

"Vintage?"

"I mean… classic?"

"You know what else is classic? Honesty. Integrity. A basic grasp of history that doesn't come from TikTack."

"It's TikTok."

"You're forty-two. That's what you said. Birth year of—let's see—1983?"

Micky licked his lips. "Yeah. Around there."

"Around there," I repeated. "How flexible is your math, Micky? Because unless you're a Doogie Howser prodigy who hit puberty at five, I'm going to need you to explain how you were the starting quarterback of a high school football team in 2013."

He had the decency to look sheepish. Or maybe that was just indigestion from the craft beer getting stuck in his throat.

"Look," Micky said, leaning forward like we were sharing a secret, "age is just a number. You're a beautiful, powerful woman. I thought you'd be flattered."

Flattered. That word. Like a match to dry kindling.

I leaned back, folding my arms. "You thought I'd be flattered that you lied to me?"

He flinched again. Probably not used to women calling the play before the snap. He wasn't a bad kid. And that was the problem. He was a kid.

"I don't do younger men. I don't need another project. I've got three grown daughters, a childish ex-husband, and a mom of my own to deal with. My quota for fixer-uppers is full."

I stood, smoothing my jacket, and gave him a smile that had closed more cases than I cared to count. "Good luck, Micky. You'll need it."

I gathered my purse, ready to chalk this up as another wasted night, but then realized that I wanted a drink. A real one. Not the polite cocktail I usually had during a date. I wanted something expensive. Something that didn't come with a side of disappointment. So instead of leaving, I sat back down.

"Micky."

He lifted his head, hopeful.

"You can go now."

He did as he was told: stood and left. He probably would've been good in bed. After I taught him what to do. That was the thing about these young whippersnappers. What they lacked in skill they made up for in enthusiasm. Or so my claw-happy cougar girlfriends told me.

I made my way to the bar, slid onto a stool, and ordered the top-shelf whiskey. Neat. No ice. No frills. I swallowed it in one gulp and delighted in the burn.

"That was the cleanest cross-examination I've seen since Brady v. Maryland."

I glanced over. Two stools down, a man sat nursing a drink, his smile edged with something dangerously close to admiration.

"Open and shut," he added, lifting his glass. "Though I'd say you gave that kid more due process than he deserved."

He was dressed like a man who knew the value of subtlety. Crisp shirt, dark blazer, no tie. The kind of man who didn't need to announce his authority because it walked into the room ahead of him.

Not a twenty-something. That much was clear. He had a wizened sort of face, full of lines that came from life. The laugh lines around his mouth had been earned, not injected. But he wasn't in his fifties, either. No gray at the temples. No softening jawline.

Could be plastic surgery, but he didn't strike me as the type to grab for the needle. He wore his skin like a man who wasn't trying to outrun time.

Still.

"Brady v. Maryland?" I repeated, tilting my head. "That case isn't even five years old."

He smiled. Lazy. Confident. "I like to stay current. And as a gentleman, I'd like to pay for your drink."

My Spidey senses were tingling. Early thirties, maybe mid. Definitely post quarter-life crisis. But also definitely not mid-life yet. Sharp enough to know his cases but not enough life behind the eyes.

He was probably a hotshot associate. Or a junior partner who thought his bar number made him a grown-up. I hadn't spent the last decade cleaning up after man-boys just to sign up for another tour of duty.

Not a candidate. But God, his smile was irritatingly watchable.

"You don't have to pay for my drink," I said, though I didn't stop him from signaling the bartender. "I can afford my own bad decisions."

"I have no doubt," he said, sliding a card onto the bar. "But as a gentleman—and a man of our profession—I feel compelled to compensate you for the floor show. That cross was textbook."

"Textbook's a stretch." I signaled to the bartender for a refill. "I skipped the impeachment step. He wasn't worth the time."

"Impeachment's only necessary when the jury's still on the fence. Your guy perjured himself with every breath. The verdict was inevitable."

This bar was my usual haunt for dates I ordered off line. It was a couple of towns over. I didn't date where I lived. Didn't drink where my neighbors could see me, either. Stillwater Springs was small-town politics wrapped in a gossip column. We had a handful of lawyers, a courthouse the size of a postage stamp, and a grapevine that worked faster than social media.

This bar was near a college. Not connected to a nightclub. Just a place where grown-ups went when they wanted to avoid craft cocktail menus and dance floors filled with twenty-somethings filming their lives for TikTok.

The types who came here were lawyers, businessmen, people who appreciated top-shelf whiskey and could afford to order it without wincing. Safe territory. Grown-up territory. No risk of running into my daughters' friends, my ex-husband's pity parties, or the client who'd think grabbing my ass after hours was "networking."

I'd never met this man. Not in court. Not at bar association mixers. Not even at the high-priced charity galas Stillwater's socialites loved to pull out a couple times a year that attracted the elites from nearby towns.

He wasn't from my business network or social network. Either way, he was still too young for my taste. You had to be at least forty years tall to ride this ride.

"Are you with one of the local firms?"

He smiled into his glass. "Something like that."

Evasive. But not defensive. Like a man who knew the value of a well-timed objection.

"I don't date where I work," I said flatly, just so we were clear.

"Good thing this isn't a date, then. This is just two professionals debriefing after a spectacular cross. You don't have to tell me your name, Coun-selor." He took a sip of his drink, that damn smile still playing at the edges. "Though I think you might want to."

Cocky. But not in the slimy way Micky had been. No, this one was dangerous. He knew exactly how far to push without overstepping.

I should've gotten up. Finished my second drink and left with my boundaries intact. But my legs had other ideas.

"You must be a defense attorney. Explains the misplaced optimism."

His grin widened. "You assume I'm still practicing."

"You assume I care."

He laughed at that—deep, warm, and far too attractive for my peace of mind.

I watched him over the rim of my glass. He had the calm of a man who'd been through enough battles to stop keeping score. He wasn't posturing. He wasn't preening. He wasn't trying to sell me on anything.

It was unnerving.

"You know," he said, tilting his head, "you're very quick to put me in a box."

"It's efficient."

"It's lazy."

That pulled a genuine laugh out of me. Damn him.

"I've earned the right to be lazy. I'm nearing fifty."

He didn't flinch.

"I run my own firm."

That got a quirk of the mouth. It said impressed, not meal ticket. Which meant he had his own money.

"And I'm tired."

He nodded as if he understood that in a way most men didn't. "Tired's fair. But lazy isn't worthy of a woman who just prosecuted a date like it was a high-profile trial. You could do better."

I downed the last of my whiskey. The burn brought me back to my senses. Though it didn't quell the ache between my legs. That was fine; I had a BOB for that. I'd stop at the convenience store on the way home to get a new pack of batteries.

"Well," I said, setting the glass down with a soft clink, "the prosecution rests."

"Case closed?"

"Closed. Filed. Motion to adjourn granted." I stood, smoothing my jacket. "The prosecution is going home to get some sleep. Alone."

He didn't move to stop me. Just tipped his glass

in a mock salute, eyes sharp with something that felt a little too much like patience. "Good night, Counselor."

He didn't chase after me. He did watch as I walked to the door. I felt his gaze on my ass and was glad my beast of a best friend had made me hold Chair Pose for an extra thirty seconds the other day. My ass did look amazing in this dress.

CHAPTER TWO

It's a special kind of irony when your daughter turns into a mirror you'd rather not look into.

Brittany—my eldest, my responsible one—was in my kitchen at 7 a.m., balancing a toddler on her hip, stirring oatmeal with her free hand, and defending her husband's late-night absence.

"He said he stayed over at a friend's house because they went out drinking."

I arched an eyebrow and took a sip of my coffee, the one small pleasure in my life that didn't expect me to pay its phone bill. "Well, yes, that is pretty responsible of Jack since he already has two DUIs."

"That was so long ago, Mom. He was still in college. We all do stupid stuff during college."

I hadn't. Neither had she. Brittany did everything right, as far as I was concerned. She got good grades and kept out of trouble. But trouble still came and found her, knocked her up, and put a ring on it. In that order.

She could've been my twin. Same tall frame, same curly blond hair hastily twisted into a bun that wouldn't survive the next hour. Same sharp cheekbones that looked good in every driver's license photo.

But where I'd softened, Brittany was still lithe. Still snatched back from childbirth like her body hadn't gotten the memo that life was supposed to slow it down. Breastfeeding and toddler-chasing had trimmed her into the version of me that existed somewhere in a dusty photograph—before courtrooms and late-night case reviews replaced playdates and stroller runs.

These days, the most running I did was pacing a courtroom floor, building a case brick by brick, question by question. Even that felt more like a controlled glide than a sprint. The only time I got my heart rate up was the occasional yoga class Tessa dragged me to, where I spent half the time wondering if my thighs would ever stop touching.

Brittany hadn't hit that phase yet. She still moved

with the urgency of someone who thought running
faster would fix the problem. I didn't have the heart
to tell her it wouldn't.

I reached for Maddie. My granddaughter didn't
come running. No squeals, no gummy grin, no
outstretched arms. Just a long, assessing look and
blue eyes that skipped right past my face and went
searching for someone better.

I swear my granddaughter huffed with resignation when Brittany passed her into my arms. A soft
little sigh like she was settling. Like I was the only
option left on the board, and she was too polite to
complain.

She always giggled when Jack's mom picked her
up on the weekends. Practically vibrated with joy.
But with me? I was the layover between her and
someone she'd rather be with.

Just like her mother.

Just like all of my daughters.

Brittany, Chloe, Emily. They all looked at me the
same way—like they were still waiting for me to be
the woman they wanted. A softer version. A version
who didn't argue. Didn't press. Didn't expect them
to stand on their own, just a bit taller, legs more
akimbo to take up more space.

I wasn't that woman who shrank. Never had

been. Not as a wife. Not as a mother. And apparently not as a grandmother either.

But in the courtroom? In the courtroom, I knew exactly who I was. I was the woman who could dismantle a hostile witness in five questions flat. The woman who could command a jury's attention, who knew how to build a case so airtight there was no escape. In court, I didn't have to be softer, quieter, easier to love. In court, I won.

I adjusted Maddie on my hip. The baby girl let me, though her eyes kept flicking to the basement door like she was counting the minutes until Grandpa made his appearance.

The basement. That was his domain in my queendom. Might as well be a dungeon. But far too much fun was being had down there. Where I had gotten my release in my bed under my own devices, my ex-husband had been in my basement having a two-person party of pleasure. I'd seen that Little Red Riding Hood sneaking out of Grandma's house early this morning.

Myles could still be the fun one. The safe one.

I was the structure. The backbone. The necessary evil.

But the thing about being the backbone is no one notices you until you break.

That was dramatic. I have never broken. And I have no intention of breaking.

I didn't break when Myles lost his job while I was pregnant with our second daughter. I didn't break while I was trying the case that made me partner in my old firm while nine months pregnant with our third baby. I didn't break when I caught Myles cheating with the nanny when he said he needed to help raise three kids as a stay at home dad.

I'd moved us back to Stillwater when I decided to open my own firm. The girls had screamed and hollered about how I was ruining their adolescent lives fifteen years ago. But I hadn't heard a peep of complaint after the designer clothes, summer cruises and holidays out of the country, or the student loan-free college and grad school.

Emily shuffled into the kitchen, eyes glued to her phone, thumbs working overtime as if the solution to her quarter-life crisis was hidden between Instagram reels and TikTok trends.

"I'm never going to amount to anything," she announced, collapsing onto a barstool like a martyr at the altar of social media. "Everyone's doing amazing things, and I'm just… static."

"You're in grad school," I pointed out, though I knew better than to expect that to help.

"Yeah, studying cultural anthropology," she groaned. "Which is basically a degree in watching other people live their lives better than me."

She scrolled aggressively, as if sheer willpower would produce a job listing for "Professional Over-thinker."

Maddie perked up in my arms, reaching for Emily with chubby, hopeful fingers. The promise of a new jungle gym.

Emily didn't notice. Or pretended not to. She was too busy watching a twenty-three-year-old "digital nomad" give a TED Talk on how she bought a villa in Italy with her Etsy sticker shop money.

Maddie huffed—yes, huffed—and slumped back against me. But then her favorite person in the world deigned to make an appearance from down below.

Once upon a time, Myles had been a rising star in software development. Now he was king of the couch cushions, always "working on something big." Which, translated, meant he was two YouTube rabbit holes away from believing he could make six figures drop-shipping novelty coasters.

My house was full of people. And not a single damn adult among them. Except me.

Myles strolled into the kitchen like he owned it,

barefoot, bed-headed, and grinning as if nothing in his life had ever been his fault. He scooped Maddie out of my arms and swung her high into the air, earning the kind of delighted squeal I hadn't been able to wring out of any of my girls their whole lives.

"There's my girl!" he crooned, pressing an exaggerated kiss to her cheek as she giggled like he'd just pulled a rabbit out of a hat.

He made the rounds, as he always did, kissing each of his daughters on the cheek like a visiting diplomat. Brittany smiled, soft and weary. Emily barely looked up from her phone.

Then he leaned in toward me. I put a hand up between us.

"Don't. I know where your mouth has been."

Myles had the audacity to smirk as he covered Maddie's ears with his hands. "Lana, we don't discuss adult business in front of the children."

The children. Like the rest of them didn't already know exactly how their father operated. Myles had been a philanderer since day one. The nanny had just been the first one I'd caught in my own house.

"You know the rules," I said, crossing my arms.

"It's not like I planned to have a guest over." Myles gave me a grin that had once gotten him out of speeding tickets. It didn't work on me anymore. "Spontaneity keeps life interesting."

"Spontaneity is going to have you sleeping in your car."

It was an empty threat. No one in this house took my words seriously. I made my escape to the only place in this house that still belonged to me. My bedroom was on the ground floor. That was by design. When I renovated, I told myself it was for convenience, for aging gracefully without stairs. The truth was, it was the farthest I could get from the circus upstairs and the man-cave in the basement. But even sanctuaries require navigation.

I stepped over two of Chloe's suitcases, shoved halfway under the hall table. A yoga mat was draped over the banister like a lazy flag of occupation. Somewhere along the way, my middle daughter had added a vintage typewriter to the collection of "treasures" she left in my house, currently perched on the sideboard like a museum exhibit no one asked for.

Chloe was my curious wanderer. Serious about nothing, passionate about everything. Until the next shiny thing caught her eye. Brittany took on everyone's burdens until she buckled. Emily collected anxieties like they were limited editions. I had no idea how I'd birthed three entirely different species.

I pushed open my bedroom door and exhaled. The bed was made. The surfaces were clean. No half-unpacked boxes. No rogue art projects. No ex-husband.

It was mine. At least for five minutes.

I crossed to the window, hoping for a brief moment of quiet, and caught sight of a woman striding up my walkway, suitcase in tow. She was gorgeous. Fit and trim. Just a little too smooth around the eyes and lips, like she had a steady relationship with her esthetician.

"Shit," I muttered, scanning the room for an escape route that didn't exist.

But there was no out. No exit strategy. Court was starting early today. And my mother was the next witness being called to the stand.

CHAPTER THREE

The sun was putting on a show over Stillwater Lake. Pink sky, gold water, the whole serenity postcard package. Just beyond the shoreline, the springs bubbled and hissed, feeding the lake with ribbons of mineral-rich water that locals swore could heal everything from heartbreak to arthritis. The air always carried a faint tang of clean, sharp, almost metallic breeze that reminded me this place had been here long before my problems, and it would outlast them too.

It was peaceful. Beautiful. The kind of place where other men found clarity and women found spiritual awakening. Me? I found reminders. That the lake was always calm on the surface but fed by restless springs underneath. A lot like me.

I sat in my car, gripping a stack of papers like they were Exhibit A in a case I was about to lose. Inside, I could hear them. Laughter, chatter, the soft buzz of women excited to be part of something. Tessa's yoga retreat center had become a mecca for girl power: book clubs, knitting circles, even a workshop on the latest in adult toy technology. Empowerment through flexibility or orgasm, you could find it all here.

Tonight, it was Celia's turn. The award-winning author was hosting a writing workshop. *Find your voice. Heal through words.* Or some such crap, my Zen bestie and my prose... let's call Celia an acquaintance. We had once been besties, but that relationship had fractured. The reason why was sitting in my lap.

I stared down at the pages that had been mocking me since I'd printed them. The last time I'd let anyone read my private thoughts, they'd left me bleeding. Figuratively. Celia hadn't meant to gut me when she said my romance novel read like a law brief. But she had. I'd retaliated with a comment sharp enough to end a friendship. That was twenty years ago.

You'd think I'd get over it by now.

But back then, that manuscript hadn't just been a

story. It had been the only space where I could breathe. I'd had two toddlers clinging to me, a husband who was slipping through my fingers, and a career that didn't care how many plates I was spinning as long as I kept them in the air.

Romance novels had been my lifeline. They'd given me things I didn't know how to ask Myles for—things I wasn't even sure he was capable of. Honesty. Vulnerability. A conversation that didn't feel like a cross-examination, where every word was a piece of evidence I had to pry out of him.

When I wrote those chapters, I wasn't just writing fiction. I was building the relationship I wished I had. So when Celia told me it lacked emotion, when she said it read like a legal brief, it didn't feel like she was critiquing my craft. It felt like she was handing me a verdict about my marriage.

It made me wonder if I'd gotten the whole damn thing wrong. My story. My suspicions. Maybe Myles wasn't cheating. Maybe I was just cold. Unloving. Maybe it wasn't him who lacked honesty. Maybe it was me who didn't know how to write it. Live it.

That seed of doubt took root. And when something takes root in you, it's hard to rip it out without tearing pieces of yourself along with it.

So no, I hadn't gotten over it. Not yet.

I didn't hear my car door open. Celia slid into the passenger seat and closed the door, shutting us in. It was the closest we'd been to each other in twenty years. It was the second time we'd been alone together in that time period, too.

She didn't say anything. Neither did I. We just sat there, the two of us, marinating in the weight of a history we were both too stubborn to dig up.

Her gaze flicked to the papers clenched in my fist. I could feel the pressure of my own grip, tight enough to leave creases. My fingers didn't loosen.

"I didn't expect you to come," she said into the quiet.

There it was. The out. The escape hatch I'd been hoping for.

But then she added quickly, as though afraid I might start the car and bolt, maybe with her in it, "I'm glad you're here. You know you're always welcome, Lana."

"Well, I had to come. My mom came to stay for the weekend. She just broke up with her latest boy toy. Or he broke up with her. I don't know."

"Oh my God, girl. Do you want to come sleep on my couch until she flies away on her broomstick?"

I chuckled at that. I also considered the offer. Only my girlfriends and I were allowed to call my mother a witch. Because Tessa and Celia knew all about Evaline's machinations.

Instead of accepting, I smoothed a hand over the papers, more to buy time than to fix the crinkles. My throat tightened, traitorous thing. I lifted my head, meeting my old friend's eyes. I could see my gaze reflected back at me in hers. Mine was vulnerable. Exposed. I hated that.

"Do you think I'm too hard to love?"

Celia's features softened in a way that felt dangerous. I felt my own harden in response. Pity wasn't an option. I would not take it. Could not take it.

But she didn't offer pity. She offered the truth.

"I love you," Celia said. No drama. No hesitation. "I've always loved you. And I've missed you every year our friendship has been broken."

I'd braced for a verdict. What I got was mercy. Mercy was a tricky thing for someone who wasn't used to it.

I didn't say anything. Words weren't my strong suit in moments like this. Instead, I tossed the pages behind me. Then I gave Celia a little chin flick. "Come on. Bring it in."

Her smile was immediate, soft and relieved. She leaned across the console and wrapped her arms around me. It was an awkward, cramped hug, but she didn't seem to care. Neither did I.

I couldn't remember the last time someone had hugged me. Tessa, probably. She was my touchy-feely bestie who'd never let me wall myself in completely. Every time I tried, she'd barge in with a hug and some hippie mantra about opening my heart chakra.

Maddie? My own granddaughter barely tolerated my hugs, squirming like she was enduring a chore before wiggling back to her mother or Myles.

But here was Celia. Celia, who knew exactly where the cracks in me were and still wanted to reach across and hold me anyway. Now with her back in my life, that made two. Two women who didn't flinch when they touched me. Double the hugs. Double the love. Or so I thought.

The yoga studio smelled like lavender and unrealistic expectations. I sat cross-legged on a cushion that felt more like a punishment than a seat, surrounded by a semi-circle of women with pages in their laps and opinions in their eyes. Tessa called it a "sacred space for creative flow." I called it a circle of judgment.

There were nine of us. Most of the women were in their forties with a few fresh-faced twenty-somethings tossed in for diversity and a couple of seasoned fifty-somethings who looked like they'd been workshopping the same memoir for the past decade.

Romance was the genre of choice tonight. A few autobiographies were sprinkled in, of course, because nothing says catharsis like reliving your worst mistakes on paper. And then there was a dark thriller that made me physically flinch. I tried to keep my face neutral, but a grimace slipped out when the hero started to stalk the heroine. Both Celia and Tessa caught it and gave me a *look*.

That look turned my grimace into a grin. I hadn't gotten a double look since high school. Ah, the band was back together again.

But now it was my turn. My pages sat in the center of the circle, freshly printed, freshly dissected. The feedback was not predictable.

"I like how mature the heroine is," one woman said, flipping through my pages like she was scanning a menu. "It's refreshing. She knows who she is."

"I agree," another chimed in. "The cougar aspect is fun."

I rolled my eyes. Cougar. As if I was prowling around for toddlers to rehabilitate. But I wasn't allowed to say anything. Celia's rule: while your work is being discussed, you shut up and listen. Torture in its purest form.

"I really enjoyed the premise," a third woman said. "But… I did feel like the writing lacked… I don't know. Emotion?"

There it was. The verdict I'd been dreading. The same one that had burned a hole in me twenty years ago.

I could feel the heat rising in my chest, but before I could turn it into a shield, Celia stepped in.

"We're still on the positive aspect of the compliment sandwich."

Yes, the compliment sandwich. We had to say something we liked about the work, followed by a critique, and end with a suggestion. For the thriller author, mine had gone something like this.

"First off, I think your pacing was something. I was on the edge of my seat the entire time. Couldn't relax for a second."

The thriller writer had smiled, missing the undertone entirely.

"That said, I am mildly concerned that you might need to be on a watchlist. Your villain's inner monologue was a little too convincing. If this is based on personal experience, we can schedule a follow-up meeting with law enforcement."

A few nervous chuckles had rippled through the group. Celia had shot me a look that said, *Stay on the rails, Lana.*

I had softened my tone, barely. "Maybe in your next draft, you can layer in a breather scene. So when the killer literally twists the knife, it cuts even deeper."

The writer nodded, scribbling furiously, as if I'd just handed her the golden key. Compliment sandwich delivered. Barely toasted but effective.

"Let's also focus on what in Lana's piece connected for you," Celia was saying now.

The group murmured. Someone mentioned liking the dialogue's rhythm. Another appreciated the heroine's dry humor. It was a half-hearted rescue attempt. I wasn't drowning just yet. Then the conversation pivoted.

"I had a note about the hero," someone said, glancing around for backup. "His dialogue felt… unrealistic. Like, no man talks like that. He says exactly what's on his mind. There's no filter. That's not how men are."

That was it. My gag order broke.

"It's a romance," I said, my voice cutting through the room like a gavel strike. "It's a fantasy. Romantic love, soul mates, happily-ever-afters—that's storybook stuff. It's not real. I know men don't say what they feel. That's why I wrote one who does. Because it's what I want. Honesty without having to cross-examine it out of him."

Silence stretched. No one quite knew what to do with that.

Celia did. She smiled gently, glancing around the circle. "And that, ladies, is the beauty of fiction. We get to write the world the way we wish it could be. Lana's heroine doesn't settle for less. Neither does her author. But it's readers that get to choose if they want to read that fantasy or not. So for next week, let's focus on reader expectations for your genre."

The circle relaxed. Pens scribbled. Pages shuffled. Crisis contained.

I wasn't sure if I wanted to thank Celia for the save… or strangle her for making me sit through it in the first place.

 unlocked the front door of the offices at 6:58 a.m. Russo & Associates wasn't a flashy firm. No marble pillars, no modern art installations pretending to mean something. The décor was simple. Clean lines, neutral tones. Orderly. Functional. Every piece of furniture had a purpose. No clutter. No wasted space. The lobby chairs were firm, not cushy, because no one needed to get comfortable in my waiting room. You came in, you got to the point, and you left.

The walls were lined with framed verdicts and settlement agreements. There were no abstract motivational posters with words like *Integrity* and *Synergy*. My work spoke for itself. I didn't need a poster to do it for me.

The whole office was mine for the first thirty minutes. Just me, the low hum of fluorescent lights, and the rhythmic tap of my heels across polished floors.

It was my favorite time of day. Everything in order. No one asking for anything. No problems yet.

At 7:30, the junior lawyers started filing in. Sharp kids. Smart enough to know the difference between hustling and flailing. They waved as they passed my office—brief, efficient, non-verbal greetings. No small talk. No chirpy weather reports. Just the way I liked it.

The paralegals weren't far behind. Organized, relentless, the backbone of every case that came through our doors. They didn't need babysitting. They needed leadership. And they had it.

By 8:00, the office was fully operational. Files exchanged hands, court schedules were double-checked, and the air had that electric crackle of a well-oiled machine humming at peak efficiency.

Anytime someone stopped by my office, it was with purpose. They stood in the doorway—not barging in—and delivered their reports with clean, surgical precision.

"Morning, Lana. Just a heads-up—the subpoena for the Keller case hit a snag. I already contacted their counsel; we're drafting a revised motion. You'll have it on your desk by ten."

"Ms. Russo, the paralegals flagged a discrepancy in the deposition transcripts. We've got two solutions. Option A is cleaner, but Option B will keep us ahead of their discovery deadlines. Your call."

That's how problems should be presented. Neatly packaged. Options in hand. No hand-holding. No drama.

This firm didn't burden me. It made me feel powerful. Every time I looked around, I saw a space that worked the way I needed it to. People who respected my time. Systems that didn't collapse without me but still knew who to come to when the final say was needed.

It was the only place in my life where I didn't have to carry everyone's load. Here, I made the calls. And no one questioned if I had the right to.

Amira Patel and Jackson Lee were my two rising stars, both gunning for the same brass ring. She was fire. He was ice. Amira came in like every conversation was a courtroom battle, always ready to swing. Jackson preferred surgical strikes, calm and precise, the assassin to her brawler.

Amira had been with me for two years, straight

out of Howard Law. Sharp mind, sharper tongue, always the first to take the fight into enemy territory. She wore power suits like armor, dark hair pulled into a sleek bun that said she had no time for nonsense.

Jackson had come from UC Berkeley. He never raised his deep, baritone voice. His words cut cleaner when they were quiet. His suits were less buttoned-up than Amira's but tailored to perfection.

Both were hungry. Both were good. They stood in my doorway—Amira with a folder clutched like a weapon, Jackson with his tablet in hand, already scrolling through something. Efficient. Respectful. My kind of people.

"We've got movement on the Jennings case," Amira started, stepping in and taking the seat closest to me. "Claire Vesper is ready for deposition prep."

Claire Vesper. Twenty-six years old. Low-level accountant turned whistleblower. She'd walked into my office six months ago with shaky hands, a USB drive, and the kind of story that made headlines.

The CEO of Jennings Dynamics, a billion-dollar tech conglomerate, had been cooking their books for years. Embezzling, laundering through fake subsidiaries, the whole buffet of corporate fraud.

Claire had found the discrepancies while working overtime no one paid her for.

When she brought it up to her supervisors, they'd responded with veiled threats, isolation, and the kind of "friendly" harassment that makes HR conveniently lose paperwork. The CEO, Richard Lyle, had taken a personal interest in keeping her quiet.

Big mistake.

"She's still nervous," Jackson said, eyes still on his tablet. "Worried about retaliation, worried about testifying. But she's solid on the facts. We've corroborated her data trails, cross-referenced with the financials from the shell companies. It's airtight."

"Good," I said, though airtight was a word I never trusted. Cases didn't breathe easy until the gavel came down.

"And we've confirmed Lyle's private asset transfers," Amira added, sliding the folder onto my desk. "He's already moving funds offshore. He knows the walls are closing in."

"He'll try to settle," Jackson said. "Or he'll try to bury Claire in legal hell."

"Let him try," I said. I'd already built her a fortress. He could bang his fists on the gates all he wanted. Claire wasn't going anywhere.

Amira smiled. Jackson didn't. He was always the more cautious of the two.

"There's one more thing," Jackson said, glancing at Amira. She gave him a nod.

"They've brought in a new defense attorney," he said. "Some hotshot from Brookhaven."

I leaned back in my chair, hands steepled under my chin. I could see they were waiting for my reaction. If this was supposed to rattle me, it didn't. No one, not even a big-city golden boy, was going to shake it loose.

"Whoever this city boy is, he'll learn soon enough whose house he's standing in."

Amira grinned. Jackson's lips twitched, which was about as close to a smile as he allowed in the office.

My phone lit up the second Amira and Jackson left.

Mom.

I considered ignoring it. Briefly. But the woman had the persistence of a process server and the moral high ground of a nun. I swiped to answer.

"When are you coming home?"

No hello. No how's your day? Straight to the point. At least I knew who I got it from.

"I'll be home when I'm done working."

"It's a shame that you're not taking care of your husband."

"We're divorced, remember? That little ceremony with the judge and the final decree? I wore white and held a bottle of expensive wine. You cried."

She ignored that, pressing on with the determination of a woman who never let facts get in the way of her narrative. "It's clear the man is trying."

I let out a short laugh. "Myles has never tried a day in his life unless it involved charming women out of their clothes."

"That's not fair, Lana. He's still here, isn't he? That means something."

"It means he knows a free ride when he sees one."

"You could show a little effort," she scolded. "Come home early. Cook the man dinner. Men like to be cared for."

"If I wanted to kill Myles, I'd do it with my cooking, and we both know it."

She huffed, the sound of a woman who refused to accept that her daughter had turned out entirely too much like herself. "I'm only trying to help you save your marriage."

"And I'm wondering when you're planning to go

back to your home," I countered, already knowing the answer.

There was a pause. Just long enough to prepare for the lie.

"I lost my apartment," she said, like it was a minor clerical error. "I was helping out Gerald. He borrowed a little too much money, but he's going to pay it back."

Gerald. That was the name this time. There was always a man. Always a story.

In the background, I heard Emily's voice, frazzled and high-pitched, complaining about something I couldn't make out. Then Myles, breezing in like the star of his own sitcom, laid on that easy charm that somehow never expired.

I did not want to go home.

"I've got another call, Mom." I didn't. But she didn't need to know that.

I hung up before she could guilt me into another lecture about how marriage was a marathon, not a sprint.

I stared at my desk. My work for the day was done. The cases were filed, the calls were made, and the fires were out. But I wasn't going home to play fixer for a family that didn't want fixing.

Instead, I opened my phone, thumbed over to the

dating app I hadn't deleted out of spite, and started scrolling. Tonight, I'd pick someone whose profile picture didn't belong to his son, whose age didn't require a permission slip.

Someone temporary. Someone easy. Hopefully, someone who actually was the age he claimed to be.

CHAPTER FIVE

J was back at my bar. Same corner booth. Same high-end bottles of well-aged spirits. Same sinking suspicion that dating apps were less about romance and more about performing social penance for existing.

Across from me sat tonight's candidate. He definitively wasn't in his thirties. He definitely wasn't in his forties either, which was still within my negotiable range. He could've been in his fifties, if I was being generous. He looked like life had taken a swing at him and didn't stop with one blow.

The man looked seventy, easy. His skin had that waxy pallor of a man who'd seen the inside of a hospital one too many times. His posture screamed chronic pain. And his eyes—oh, his eyes. They scanned me like I was the next home health aide on his insurance plan. We hadn't even made it to drink orders before he started with the questions.

"Do you have good health insurance?" he asked as if we were conducting a job interview for an in-home nurse. "PPO or HMO?"

I took a sip of my whiskey, which he'd put on his tab. "I run my own law firm. And I offer my employees excellent coverage."

I was expecting a jab at my profession or a dig at being a professional woman or a veiled inquiry about the hours I kept.

Instead, I got "Do you know CPR?"

That was new. I was almost too amused to get up and end this train wreck. But the only place I had to go was home. Tessa was teaching a yoga class. Celia was on a date with her next-door-neighbor-with-benefits. So no girlfriends were coming to my rescue.

"I do know CPR."

My date nodded as though checking an item off his list in the pro column.

"Just know that if you drop dead right now, I will be charging you for billable hours."

His chuckle was a phlegmy, wheezy sound that made me reach for my drink again.

"I can take care of you, you know." He puffed up his chest like he was still the catch he'd once been. "Financially. I've done well for myself. You'd never have to worry about money again."

The way he said it, like it was a dangling carrot, made me want to laugh.

Money was never the problem. What I needed was someone who didn't see me as an investment, period. Not for a meal ticket. Not for their end-of-life care. Someone who didn't look at me like a solution to their declining mobility and expired prescriptions.

"I'm not in the market for a sugar daddy."

He blinked, surprised. Like no woman had ever turned down the privilege of rubbing his back with Bengay and monitoring his blood pressure.

I had submitted a dating profile for his review, not a resumé. Still, he was treating it as a job interview, not a date.

"I just know you're the kind of woman I need in my life." He leaned in, oblivious to the fact that I was physically leaning away. "Strong, reliable, nurturing—"

"Nurturing is definitely not my brand," I said, dousing the statement with sarcasm. He didn't notice. Or didn't care.

"You'll come around," he said like that was a promise, not a threat, "once you see how well I'll take care of you. You won't have to worry about rent, bills, none of that stress. I've got a nice house, plenty of space. I'll never cheat on you. You'll always know where I am. I'm a homebody. The only time I'd be out is for a doctor's appointment."

He paused, his gaze narrowing like he was making a very important life decision.

"You drive, right?"

I was calculating the least confrontational way to escape without creating a scene—fake phone call, emergency text, spontaneous case of food poisoning—when a shadow fell over our table.

"I see you've met my ex-wife," a familiar voice drawled. Smooth, amused, utterly unapologetic.

I looked up and up. It was him. The man from the last disaster of a date. It was the first time I'd seen him standing. He was tall. He was also wearing that damnable grin that made it hard to decide if I wanted to thank him or punch him.

My elderly date—or interviewer—blinked. "Ex-wife?"

My bar buddy slid into the booth next to me like he belonged there with his arm draped across the back casually, his tone conspiratorial. "Oh yeah. Best mistake I ever made. But let me warn you—she's got a bit of a… high-octane lifestyle."

I turned my head slowly, raising a brow. He ignored me.

"She trains for marathons," he continued, leaning toward the older man. "At 4 a.m. Every day. Never misses a session. Very intense."

The older man's brows furrowed.

"And she's a competitive salsa dancer on week-ends," he added, dropping that with a straight face. "Trophies and everything."

I coughed into my glass to cover the snort. But my rescuer wasn't done.

"Also, she's a bit of an adrenaline junkie. Last time I saw her, she was talking about BASE jumping in the spring."

The old man's complexion had gone several shades paler.

"Lovely woman," my young protector said, giving my shoulder a light, conspiratorial squeeze. "But I gotta warn you, she's not the stay-at-home, cozy-on-the-couch type. More of a 'let's ride motorcycles across the Andes' kind of gal."

That did it. The older man mumbled something about an early morning and shuffled out like his life depended on it.

My new dinner companion waited until he was out the door before turning to me, his expression infuriatingly smug. "You're welcome."

I stared at him, deadpan. "I don't salsa."

"You could," he said, standing up and offering me his hand. "But let's start with a drink. You owe me one."

"You lie very well."

"To save a pretty woman's life? Yeah, I'd lie through my teeth. I was a Boy Scout." He held up his hand with three fingers raised.

I reached up and lowered one of his fingers to resemble the Cub Scout pledge. "I doubt you're old enough to be a Boy Scout."

He chuckled at that, looking at me with delight. "Says the woman who first brought a cub out for a date and then a dying hyena. That dude almost hacked up a lung."

I couldn't help myself; I laughed. The night had been a series of absurdities. Laughing was the most natural response to it.

"I'm buying you another round," said my savior.

"I'm not going home with you."

"I don't live here."

"I have no interest in being a nurse or a purse."

That made him grin. "I'm buying you a drink.

And I'm at the prime of my physical fitness. So neither of those descriptors applies to me."

I glanced down at his body. He wore his shirt well—fitted but not painted on. Broad shoulders, trim waist. The kind of build that said he didn't skip leg day, but he wasn't spending his life flexing in a mirror, either. His forearms were solid, corded with lean muscle, not the puffed-up kind that screamed midlife crisis.

No wedding ring. No fade of a band on his ring finger. Strong hands. Relaxed but not sloppy. Confident in that quiet way that didn't need validation. His jaw had the start of a five o'clock shadow, not from laziness, but from a man who'd had a full day of actually doing something.

Prime of his physical fitness? I wasn't going to give him that. Out loud. But he wasn't wrong.

"Since I'm not asking you to take care of me financially, medically, or sexually, I am in no way stepping on your autonomy."

So wait. Was he not attracted to me?

He chuckled again like he could read my mind. "Trust me, I wouldn't say no to the third option. If it ever became an option."

Him saying the words out loud made it an option in real time.

"You are the most breathtaking woman I have ever met."

I didn't do that thing when women tried to demure and detract from their attractiveness. I knew I looked good. Not just for my age. I looked good, period.

And so did he. He smelled good too. Felt good as well. I knew because of that light touch on my shoulder. Even then, he hadn't taken any liberties. Only a featherlight touch to scare off the other guy. But as soon as that man was gone, so was his touch. He'd even slid over a bit to give me back more of my personal space.

"Tell me about you," he said as the waiter set another drink in front of me.

"Why?"

"Because it's the second time you've been here with a man, but neither of them asked any personal questions while I was eavesdropping."

"So you admit you were eavesdropping."

"I absolutely was. I wanted some ammunition to use when they both inevitably bombed."

"You were so sure they were going to bomb?"

"Absolutely. Those eyes told me how intelligent you were. Those lips that kept smirking at them told me you had a sense of humor. But you're not cruel.

And the way your nostrils flared when they pissed you off told me you have a lot of unspent desire in you. So I waited patiently while they bombed, hoping to sneak in and claim you for myself."

I gaped at him, my mouth set in a line that probably looked unimpressed. It wasn't.

"That's a hell of a cross-examination," I said, my voice steady, even as my pulse betrayed me. "You built that whole case just by watching me suffer through a bad date?"

"Two bad dates." He leaned in, just enough to make my breath catch. "I'm very observant."

"I bet you are." I sipped my drink mostly to buy time. "But here's the thing about cases. Just because you read the evidence doesn't mean you get the verdict you want."

His grin didn't falter. "I'm prepared to appeal."

"I am not sleeping with you."

He only grinned and took another sip of his drink.

CHAPTER SIX

"One night," I insisted.

"Sure," he said as he slammed the door of the hotel room shut, then slammed me up against it.

We barely made it inside before his mouth found mine again, insistent and sure, as if he'd been waiting all night to shut me up. I let him.

"I assume this means you'll tell me your name now," he murmured against my lips, his hands already working their way under my jacket.

"No." I tugged his shirt free from his waistband. "I don't want anything from you but your body."

"Fair trade." He didn't miss a beat. His mouth found my neck, and my jacket hit the floor.

"I'm Theo," he said, pulling back just enough to

meet my eyes. "Figured you should know what name to call out as I'm balls deep inside you."

That made me laugh, a sharp, surprised sound that felt foreign in my own throat. I couldn't remember ever laughing during sex. Not in the kind of way that felt like… fun.

Theo grinned like a man who'd won a round I didn't know I was playing. "I guess I'll be calling you God."

Another laugh. This one lighter, unexpected. He was ridiculous. And for the first time in a long time, I didn't mind being in the middle of ridiculousness.

Theo lifted me like I weighed nothing and set me down on the bed. My blouse was gone. My slacks, too. I sat there in my bra and underwear, legs crossed, arms loose at my sides, waiting to see if reality was going to catch up and ruin this.

He stood a few feet away, eyes scanning my body. I wasn't twenty-five. My thighs had opinions. My belly had stories. I was fit, yes—but life had left its fingerprints.

Theo didn't flinch. But he did turn. For a half-second, I thought; *Here it comes*. The polite exit. The too-sudden text from his buddy. Instead, he walked to the other side of the room and flipped on the coffeemaker.

"What are you doing?" I sat up in the bed, too confused to hide my flaws.

"Making you coffee." He said it like it was the most obvious thing in the world. "You've had two drinks. I want you sober for what we're about to do."

Theo looked over his shoulder, eyes dark with promise. The nerve of this man.

He wasn't in a rush. Wasn't trying to get his before the clock ran out. He was… preparing. Making sure I was present. Awake. Not hiding behind a buzz.

It rattled me more than a cheap line ever could. I didn't want him to see that. So I sat back, crossing my arms over my chest. "This a regular thing for you? Caffeine and foreplay?"

"Only with women I don't want to forget."

Damn him for that. Now I definitely wouldn't forget him either.

"How do you take it?" he asked, holding the mug like it was a challenge.

"Black," I said. "The way life serves it."

His grin spread slow and lazy. "Figured as much."

That earned him a raised brow. "Oh? And what exactly does that mean?"

Theo didn't miss a beat. "You're a no-nonsense,

no-frills kind of woman. You like things strong and straight to the point. I like that."

He brought the cup to me, careful and deliberate, as if handing over a loaded weapon.

I scooted to the edge of the mattress, planting my feet on the floor, to accept the offered beverage.

Then without ceremony, he knelt in front of me.

Not a grand gesture. Not some worshipful display. He just settled between my legs, as if that was his place. As if it had been all along.

"Drink," he said, his voice smooth, even as his hands gently coaxed my thighs apart.

I lifted the cup to my lips out of defiance more than thirst. The first sip was hot, bitter, and grounding. It curled through my chest, warming me from the inside out.

Theo's mouth found the inside of my thigh. The contrast was electric.

The coffee was heat—but steady, controlled, something I could brace against. His lips were molten. They branded, teased, lingered. Every press of his mouth sparked against the nerves the coffee had only just begun to wake.

I took another sip, this time slower, as if that could anchor me. But his mouth was already charting its course, inch by maddening inch, up my inner thighs. My breath was starting to betray me. The heat from the coffee settled in my belly. His mouth made sure it didn't stay there.

"Keep drinking," he murmured against my skin, his lips brushing a spot at the crease of my inner thighs that made my legs tense. "I'm just getting started."

And that was the problem.

So was I.

"Theo," I sighed.

"Yes, God?"

Again, I cracked a smile. "It's Lana. You can call me Lana."

"Can I suck your clit, Lana?"

"Yes, Theo."

And then he did. I set the coffee down rather than spill it. The cup wasn't empty, but I was completely sober.

Theo tongued me like he was making an argument. My body talked back. But it didn't argue. It was in complete agreement with this man. I was mortified by the hungry, wet sounds my body was making, but the hell would I tell him to stop.

I came embarrassingly fast. And hard. So hard I couldn't hold my upper body up and flopped back onto the mattress.

In my defense, it had been a long time since I'd had oral sex. Most guys from dating apps didn't offer it on the first meeting, and I was rarely interested in a second date. Likely because my favorite sexual act hadn't been served up.

But Theo? He rose from his perch on the ground like he'd just warmed up and was gearing up for round two.

"Do you want soft or hard, Lana?"

I blinked, still half in a daze from that orgasm. My body was still clenching around aftershocks.

Soft or hard? No one had ever asked me beforehand. They might ask if it was too hard. No, actually I hadn't been asked that either. Now I was being given a choice.

"Both."

Theo grinned like it was the right answer. He grabbed my unfinished coffee and took a sip. He licked the rim where my lipstick had left an impression. Then he licked his lips, as though swallowing down every taste he could get of me.

He stood at the edge of the bed like he had all the time in the world. I sure as hell didn't. I'd spent most of mine taking care of everyone else. But right then, with Theo in front of me, I wanted every second stretched out until it snapped.

His hands went to his shirt, slow and deliberate like he was cross-examining me with each button. I let my eyes track the movement, unapologetic. A woman my age has earned the right to ogle. The fabric slid off his shoulders and revealed muscle, lean and hard. His chest was broad enough to cast shadows across his ribs, and I wanted to follow every line with my mouth, map him like he was a case file I needed to memorize.

Scars interrupted the perfection—thin white lines scattered like punctuation. My gaze dipped lower as he dropped his pants. I'd told myself he was too young. But watching him now, shedding each piece of armor, I knew I'd lied. He wasn't a boy. Every inch of him was man, and I wanted all of it.

Once he was dressed in nothing but a condom, he came to the bed. He climbed over top of me and entered me slowly, gently. The head of his cock asked permission with each inch—and there were a lot of inches. I gave way as he fucked me softly, as promised.

I think both of us felt my muscles tightening, preparing for a second orgasm. That's when he started to fuck me hard. Then harder. It was like his body was calling my orgasm to the witness stand. For a minute, my orgasm was a hostile witness. She wasn't used to being called for a redirect. But Theo was insistent.

He and that deliciously thick dick of his battered my core over and over again. Fast thrusts. Slow circles. But always, always hard.

His hands clamped down on my hips, not letting me get away. Not letting me retreat. Not letting me hide behind any defenses.

I did the only thing I could do. I came. And came and came.

At some point, I noticed that his thrusts had stopped, and he was slumped over me. Chest heaving. Breaths coming quick. He still had a tight hold on me. I'd likely sport some bruises in the morning.

I didn't mind his weight. Which was an odd thing for me to realize. I was a straw of hay away from my back breaking. But he lifted off me and curled himself around my back.

"I can't stay the night," I warned once my breathing was back to normal.

"Okay. Don't wake me when you leave. I'll probably be dreaming about you, and I don't want to be interrupted from the truly dirty things I'll be doing to dream-you."

"What we just did wasn't dirty?"

"That was tame. That was first-fuck behavior.

You have no idea what kind of fuckery we'll get up to on the second fuck. I'd be happy to show you if you come back."

I bit my lip, deciding how to respond to that.

"Go to sleep, Lana. Or pretend to. Then sneak out when I'm asleep."

That's exactly what I did.

CHAPTER SEVEN

"*I*s everyone getting laid but me?"

Tessa set down her almond milk chai and gave us both a look. It was the kind of look that turned into a smirk before it even fully formed.

"You two are glowing."

Celia coughed into her cup, but she didn't deny it. No one would believe any denial from her lips since everyone on her block saw her sneaking over to Bo Porter's house each night and doing—well, not exactly a walk of shame in the morning. It was more of a twirl of satisfaction in the early morning light.

I just arched a brow at Tessa's observation. I might not have twirled out of Theo's hotel room in the middle of the night, but I had been grinning. Not a single shameful thing happened between those sheets.

If I were being honest, I was contemplating a second time. What had he called it? A first-fuck. And man, I was jonesing for some second sin. The devil on my shoulder wasn't whispering for me to go back; she was stomping her hooves and shaking her horns in demand.

"At least I have inner peace," Tessa added, waving her hands between her brows and her heart, indicating her Zen. "And a very reliable showerhead."

I snorted into my espresso. Celia cracked up. The three of us devolved into the kind of laughter that made your face ache and your mascara betray you.

We sat at the corner table of Bean There, Done That talking about having our beans diddled. The place was part nostalgia, part caffeine, and all comfort. The coffee shop had chipped tile floors that had seen more than one generation of bad decisions and more heart-to-hearts than chairs. The same faded yellow walls had held protest flyers in the nineties, poetry slams in the aughts, and now, in its middle age, it was a haven for women like us— women who were wise enough to know better but reckless enough to ignore it, anyway.

"Okay, but seriously—" Tessa leaned forward,

grinning. "Someone tell me something juicy. I haven't had sex in years."

The love of Tessa's life had passed away a few years ago. Tessa hadn't even considered dating. She'd been far too busy mourning the amazing man her husband had been.

Instantly, Celia and I sobered.

"No, do not feel sorry for me. Talk dirty to me."

"Well, I have never had so many orgasms in my life," Celia offered. "I rarely had any over the last twenty years. And now, in a matter of weeks, Bo has made my legs shake so much I thought it was the start of arthritis."

Tessa held up her hand for a high-five. Celia smacked it and did a little shimmy with her shoulders.

From the corner, the familiar rustle of newspaper snapped through the air like a disapproving nun's ruler. Old Man Wendell, corner table, seat by the heater vent, same time every Tuesday. He shook out his *Stillwater Gazette* like it personally offended him, even though he hadn't turned the page since we sat down twenty minutes ago.

I didn't even bother to look his way. "If you didn't like what you were hearing, Mr. Wendell, you'd find a new place to loiter."

He grunted. Didn't move. Didn't flip the page. He'd been eavesdropping on our sex lives for weeks.

"Mm-hmm," I muttered, "that's what I thought."

Tessa winked at him. Celia took a long, slow sip of her cappuccino.

We weren't girls anymore. We didn't whisper in corners or keep our wants folded into tiny, polite pockets. We ordered drinks we liked, said things out loud, and dared the world—or Wendell—to flinch.

"All right, Russo. Spill it. Clearly, the latest Tinder date wasn't a disappointment."

I took a long, strategic sip of coffee and set the mug down with the weight of resignation. "He asked if I had CPR certification and decent health insurance before the drinks arrived."

Celia winced. Tessa gagged. Wendell turned the page.

"Total bust," I confirmed. "But… afterwards, I hooked up with a guy I met at the bar."

Celia blinked. Tessa dropped her croissant. Wendall put the newspaper down.

"I'm sorry—what?" Celia leaned in like I'd just announced a crime. "You hooked up? With a stranger?"

"I didn't say he was a stranger. I'd seen him there before. We'd chatted after another app disappointment. Then he rescued me from the old geezer who wanted a nurse."

"That is something we would've done in our twenties," Tessa said. "Or maybe thirties if we were drunk enough."

"I definitely wasn't drunk." I thought about the coffee Theo had made me drink as he drank from me.

"You don't usually do repeats," said Tessa. "But you saw this guy twice and slept with him? Lana Russo, are you in a relationship?"

"Hardly. The guy is in his thirties."

Tessa gasped, slapping the table.

Celia looked between us. "I don't get it."

Tessa turned to Celia, full of exaggerated scandal. "Lana doesn't date men under forty-five. She calls them children. Says she doesn't need to raise anyone else."

Celia's head bobbed in agreement with that statement. Then her gaze turned quizzical. "Sounds like this thirty-year-old took care of you last night."

Wendell gave his newspaper another aggressive snap.

"Will you see him again?" Celia asked.

I opened my mouth to say no. To rattle off the usual line: one night only, no strings, no mess. But then I thought about the way Theo looked at me. Like he saw the gears turning in my head and still wanted in. About how he hadn't asked a single thing from me but had given so much—his attention, his touch, his name.

He hadn't been a burden. He'd been a damn relief. He hadn't even tried to hold on to me. He'd let me go.

The truth was, I'd had a hard time leaving after he fell asleep. The truth was, I wanted to go back. Not to fix anything, not to hold anyone together. But to be held.

That thought stopped me cold.

Wanting to take care of someone had always been the first red flag. But this… didn't feel like that. It felt like something else. Like I had more room to breathe with him. Because he'd carved out space for me.

Which was probably why I couldn't let it happen again.

I shook my head and stood, grabbing my bag. "I'm going to throw myself into this whistleblower case. Burn the midnight oil, win the damn thing."

Tessa frowned. "You'll at least give him a call?"

"Nope," I said, popping the 'p.' "I didn't get his number. All I know is where he's staying—for now.

But after I win this case? After I walk out of that courtroom with justice on my side, maybe then I'll go see if he's still there."

He wouldn't be. A young guy like that, who actually knew what he was doing with the thing in his pants, wouldn't wait around for anyone. Much less an older woman like me.

CHAPTER EIGHT

The courthouse steps were cracked and crooked, like everything else in this town that hadn't been updated since dial-up. I climbed them anyway, heels steady, spine straighter than I felt. It was too early for a headache and too late to turn back.

Inside, Amira and Jackson were already circling each other like caffeinated hawks. She was buttoned up brilliance in a sharp blazer and heels that meant business. He was smug charm in rolled-up sleeves and a tie already loose at the neck. I watched them trade barbs over a misfiled subpoena and a coffee run that hadn't happened. Neither of them noticed me at first. They were too busy pretending they didn't care about impressing the other.

I resisted the urge to roll my eyes and instead cataloged the moment for later. Celia would eat this up. Enemies to lovers. Office romance. She'd probably have them in a supply closet by chapter three. I'd send her the blueprint if I had time. Or if I still believed in that kind of thing for myself. My own romance novel dreams had been buried somewhere between the first time I found another woman's panties in my laundry to the time I found a naked woman in the backseat of my husband's car, sitting reverse cowgirl on my husband.

Still, I liked the rhythm of words. Maybe I'd write something someday. Something where the older woman gets the silver-haired fox and doesn't have to cook him dinner or iron his ego. You know—pure fantasy.

Amira spotted me first. "You're early."

Jackson lifted a hand in mock salute. "We were just keeping the hallway warm for you."

They flanked me as we moved through security and into the bowels of the courthouse. Somewhere in these beige-painted corridors was justice. And our star witness.

"We got eyes on the new defense attorney," Jackson said as we walked. "He's already in the building."

Amira nodded. "Young. Sharp. Polished like a campaign ad."

"Handsome, too," Jackson added, making me doubt my shipping of him and Amira. But this generation of young men didn't appear to have a problem complimenting each other. Likely to do with the whole everyone gets a trophy phenomenon.

"He's got a reputation. Came from a firm in Chicago," Amira said. "Very high-profile, very connected."

I used to be high profile and connected. Didn't stop my winning record when I left the big city to work in my hometown. Didn't stop my ex-husband from sleeping with the family therapist, either.

We turned down the final corridor, and my heels echoed louder than anything else in the silence. Let the golden boy be brilliant. Let him be charming. Let him have a jawline sharp enough to cut glass on. He still had to go through me. And I didn't flinch for pretty faces or padded résumés.

Claire Vesper was waiting in the witness room, her hands twisted together in her lap. She was twenty-five. Smart. Wrecked. Courage was leaking through the cracks in her fear. I stepped inside and gave her the version of myself that didn't terrify people.

"Claire," I said gently, sliding into the chair beside her. "You holding up?"

She looked at me with wide, haunted eyes. "I didn't sleep."

"I rarely do," I told her. "It's overrated."

That got me a small smile. I'd take it.

"You're about to walk into a room where they'll try to make you feel like the problem. They'll question your memory, your motives, your integrity. But not once will they question the man who made you feel like you had no choice but to speak up."

Claire swallowed hard.

"You're not alone in this. I'm with you. Amira and Jackson are with you. You're doing something brave. And I don't let brave people fall."

Claire blinked fast, like she might cry. But she didn't. She nodded instead. "I just want to do the right thing."

"We will," I said. "Now let's go ruin a CEO's day."

The courtroom smelled like over-polished wood and stale ambition. I'd been in this room more times than I could count. It always felt the same. Cool, formal, humming with restrained nerves. The flags never moved. The walls always watched. The floor creaked in the same spots.

I knew this space better than my own living

room. Knew the layout, the rhythm, the rules. Knew the bailiff, the court reporter, even the janitor, who always left a faint trail of lemon-scented floor wax in his wake. This room didn't rattle me. I'd won more than I'd lost in here. I planned to add another W to the tally by the end of this case.

There were only two judges on this circuit. Judge Lipman had taken the sabbatical he'd been threatening for years—fishing in Florida, last I heard. That left Judge Bellamy. Old-school, deliberate, fair. He was retiring soon, but I was glad we'd pulled him for this one. I knew how he thought. Knew how to frame this case so it would hit all his pressure points. This case was about power, corruption, and corporate cruelty. Judge Bellamy hated bullies.

The defense filed in just before the clock struck. I didn't look at them right away. I clocked the scent of too much cologne and the sharp clip of loafers that cost more than my first car. A male voice laughed self-satisfied. I glanced up just in time to catch a set of broad shoulders and dark, styled hair. Whoever he was, he had the self-importance of a man who expected the world to part for him like the Red Sea.

He turned—and smiled.

A dazzling, too-white grin aimed itself straight at me like a weapon. Botoxed forehead, teeth that gleamed like a toothpaste commercial, and just enough smirk to make me want to call for backup. He looked like every bad lawyer stereotype rolled into one. Too polished, too rehearsed, too pleased with himself.

He crossed to me with a hand outstretched. I stood only because I'm not rude in public. Or at least not without cause.

"Archibald Stalworth, Esquire," he said like he was offering royalty, not a handshake.

His hand was cold. His nails too long. The kind of man who moisturized but forgot to clip. I wanted to shudder.

"We'll keep this civil, I'm sure," he said with a wink.

I gave him the kind of tight smile I usually reserve for tax auditors and dental hygienists with bad breath.

The bailiff's voice cut in like a knife. "All rise."

I turned, filing toward our table with Amira and Jackson, my mind already shifting into courtroom mode. I didn't see the judge enter. I didn't need to. I knew the routine. We stood, we waited, we sat. But then—

"Ladies and gentlemen, there's been a change.

Judge Bellamy had a medical emergency and has been admitted to the hospital."

That voice—

That voice had made me moan into a hotel pillow last night.

That voice had told me I was beautiful as its owner slid inside of me and made me forget the world.

"I've been asked to step in and take over the case. I'm Judge Theo Marsden."

My spine locked. I lifted my head slowly. And there he was. On the damn bench. In the damn robe.

His eyes found mine. Recognition hit us both at the same time.

Judge Theo Marsden.

God help me.

Because I'd called him God. Out loud. More than once.

And now?

He was presiding over my case.

CHAPTER NINE

'd been in enough courtrooms to know when someone was looking at me like I'd already lost. Theo—Judge Marsden—wasn't looking at me like that. He was looking at me like I was still naked.

It was one thing to feel that look in a hotel room two towns over. It was quite another thing to feel it under the buzzing lights of a courtroom with a defense attorney, my staff, the bailiff, and the clerk watching. I'd never felt so exposed in my life—and I've given closing arguments on two hours of sleep in a suit that smelled faintly of vomit from my youngest's flu.

Theo's eyes shuttered once, like his brain needed a reset before he came back online. The heat in his gaze vanished, replaced with the sober realization that I was the prosecutor.

"In my chambers. Now."

For one foolish heartbeat, I thought maybe we'd pick up where we left off last night. The heat, the recklessness, the way his hands had mapped me like I was both a puzzle and the prize for solving it. I could still feel the press of him against me, the rasp of his stubble on my neck, the way my laugh had slipped out at the wrong moment and turned into a moan when he refused to let me wriggle away. The way he'd held me down with one hand, as if daring me to stop him, while with the other he'd coaxed out every last ounce of fight until I wasn't fighting at all. Until I was begging. Until my brain—always so damn busy calculating, fixing, controlling—had finally gone silent.

But then Archibald stepped back from the defense table. He made a motion with his hands for me to precede him. This wasn't a party of two in his chambers; it was the court's business with counsel.

Reality returned like a brick to the head. If I recused myself, I'd have to say why. And I'd have to say it in front of Archie.

The doors shut behind us. Theo stood behind the big oak desk, calm, collected. Every inch the judge, not the thirty-something who'd made me laugh and moan and beg until I forgot where I was last night.

Archibald folded his arms across his chest. "I know what this is about."

He did? My pulse spiked so hard I felt it in my teeth. Heat shot up my neck, prickling under my collar, while my stomach did the kind of drop you get when the elevator jerks. My palms went slick. I could see it—front page of the *Stillwater Gazette,* whispered about over wine at every book club in town: *Prosecutor Sleeps with Judge Before Trial.* The kind of gossip that would stick to my name longer than any legal victory.

"Theo and I have history. But we can both be impartial. No need to recuse."

Oh. That was Archie's story. His history with Theo. Not mine.

I exhaled slowly, hoping it didn't sound like relief.

Theo glanced at me. I swallowed hard. This was my out. Archibald's admission meant I could keep my mouth shut and avoid turning this into courtroom gossip before the trial even began.

But ethics are a nasty little parasite. It lived under my skin, scratching, reminding me they were there. I could lie by omission. But it would gnaw at me. Likely for the rest of my life.

I opened my mouth to confess. Theo beat me to it.

"The law matters," he said evenly. "We have to do what's best for the parties involved. I'm going to call the court administrator and recuse myself from the case due to… personal matters."

Archibald huffed, like ethics were just another scheduling inconvenience.

I stayed silent, still facing forward.

Theo reached for the office phone. It was an actual phone, complete with a cord plugged into the base like it was 1995. He punched in a number. I watched his fingers move over the buttons. They were quick and confident. I had the ridiculous thought: *Does he even know how to work one of these? Did they have rotary phones when he was a kid? Is he that young?*

Apparently not because he didn't fumble once on the dial. He caught me looking. Those sharp eyes flicked up, catching me mid-speculation. I cleared my throat and looked away, studying a very interesting patch of wall.

The phone rang. And rang. And rang.

Finally, a woman's voice exploded through the

receiver. Breathless, harried, and clearly halfway through chewing someone out before Theo's call interrupted her. I could practically hear the papers hitting the desk. "Court administration."

"This is Judge Marsden. I'm going to need to recuse myself from the Jennings Dynamics case."

There was a sharp inhale on the other end. "Now? You've been on the docket for five minutes."

"Yes," Theo replied evenly. "I have a prior relationship with both counselors."

The word *relationship* hung in the air like a loaded gun. Archibald's eyes slid toward me. I didn't move. Didn't blink. If I stayed perfectly still, maybe he couldn't see me if I didn't move.

Thankfully, the administrator didn't ask what kind of relationship. Though I did wonder what Theo's relationship with Archie had been. Likely professional. Maybe they were frat brothers. Or in the same kindergarten class together.

On the other end, the woman's voice snapped back, sharp and impatient. "Judge Bellamy's out for six weeks after his surgery. Every other judge in the circuit's got a docket stacked to the ceiling. You're it, Marsden."

Archibald actually fist-pumped the air, like this

was the best news since the invention of billable hours.

Theo didn't react to him. He just lifted his gaze to mine, steady, searching. It wasn't the cocky look from last night. It wasn't the professional mask he'd worn walking into chambers. It was something else —something that felt like a question: *Are you okay with this? With me?*

And damn him, it was the kind of question that made my chest go warm and my stomach sink at the same time. Because he wasn't just asking for his own sake. He was asking for mine.

It made me want to say *yes*. It made me want to believe there could be something here, something worth starting between us. But it also made the truth impossible to ignore.

It wasn't okay.

"I'll recuse," I said, breaking the silence.

Archibald smirked, like he'd just won the whole case.

The administrator's response was instant and cutting. "Counselor Russo? No, you won't. You can't. You're the only prosecutor in the district certified for this whistleblower statute. Unless you've got a twin in the hallway ready to step in, you're staying right where you are."

I looked back at Theo, helpless. I'd never looked at a man like I was helpless. I always had the answers, the next move, the way out. Theo returned my gaze like he was already working the problem, like he was going to fix it for me.

The court administrator's voice cut through the line. "Is anything personal going on currently between either counselors and the judge?"

Archibald jumped in before Theo or I could breathe. "No. Judge Marsden and I used to work at the same firm back in Chicago. But that was years ago, and we haven't seen each other since."

Theo's eyes shifted to me. In that look, I could feel it—the slow, inevitable swing of a door closing. Not slamming. Just drifting shut, the way something does when you know it's over before it ever had a chance to begin.

Which was exactly what I wanted, right? I didn't do relationships. I was married to my career.

Theo didn't answer. He let me do it.

"No," I said, the word flat on my tongue. "There's currently nothing personal going on between myself and Judge Marsden."

Something in me caved in. Hollowed out. Like a firework I'd lit with fingers trembling with anticipation, only to watch it sputter, hiss, and die in the dark without ever reaching the sky.

My chest felt too wide, my ribs scraped raw, as though the words themselves had taken a crowbar to me. I had just erased us. With one syllable. Wiped out every spark, every laugh, every whispered plea from last night and shoved it into some nameless drawer labeled irrelevant.

"Good," the administrator replied without missing a beat. "Then get back to work."

The line went dead.

Theo's expression didn't change. Unreadable. Like last night hadn't happened.

Which was fine. I'd already been planning to keep my distance. I didn't have the time, the energy, or the stupidity to fall for a man ten years younger—especially one in a black robe who could wreck my career.

I'd just have to keep my eyes off him. And my mind off the fact that the last time I'd been in a room alone with Theo Marsden, the only thing between us had been the steam from a cup of coffee and his mouth between my thighs.

CHAPTER TEN

"For the record, the court went into chambers to discuss potential recusals. I disclosed to the court administration that I have had prior dealings outside the courtroom with both counselors. All parties were made aware, and due to exceptional circumstances—no replacement judge available—I will proceed."

Theo's eyes didn't touch mine. Not once. We didn't have to pretend we were complete strangers. We did have to acknowledge that we would no longer be intimate partners, which was almost believable if you ignored the fact that I'd had my hands in his hair twelve hours ago while he… Well. Let's just say my dealings with him outside the courtroom had been considerably more thorough than anything that had happened with Archibald.

"Do either the defendant or the witness have any issues with this arrangement?"

From the table beside me, I felt Amira's and Jackson's stares—sharp with unspoken questions. What had just happened in chambers was highly irregular, and they knew it. I didn't have answers for them. I didn't have eyes for them either. My focus was locked on Claire.

Claire turned toward me. Her expression was part question, part prayer. There was a time I relished being a god to my clients, the one with all the answers. Well, all the answers to this case at least.

I took a breath. It settled in my ribs and dared me to make a different choice. "No," I answered, clear and steady. "We've got a rock solid case. I'm going to win it, no matter who the judge or the defense attorney is."

Something loosened in Claire's shoulders. She gave me a little nod—confidence borrowed from me, handed back in trust.

When I looked up at Theo, the man looking back was all business. His expression could have been carved from the bench itself. For a moment, that got to me. Made me wonder if I'd imagined the sadness in his eyes earlier, when that imaginary door on our… whatever it was… had slowly closed.

Maybe there hadn't been sadness at all. Maybe he'd been relieved he wasn't going to have to break it off with me. The thought hit harder than it should have.

He adjusted the papers in front of him, the picture of judicial neutrality. "Counselor, you may proceed."

This wasn't a jury trial—whistleblower cases in this circuit rarely were. Too complicated, too technical for jurors to stay awake through, never mind understand. The judge was the fact-finder here. Which meant my rock-solid case was going to live or die entirely in the hands of the man I'd spent the night with. The man who wasn't looking at me right now.

I rose from my chair, the weight of every eye in the room sliding over me like a silk sheet with teeth. This was where I shone. My back straightened, and my head tilted back like the weight of the invisible crown on my head was no sweat.

"May it please the court," I began, voice steady. "This case is about truth. About the courage it takes for one person to stand up against the kind of corporate greed that doesn't just bend the rules—it grinds them into dust."

Claire sat at the prosecution table, hands clasped in her lap. She looked smaller than usual, but her spine was straight. I took a step toward the bench, the rhythm of my words like the click of a metronome.

"The defendant, Mr. Richard Lyle, was the CEO of Jennings Dynamics. Mr. Lyle is a man who was trusted with the livelihoods of hundreds of employees. A man who was paid a salary that would take most of us ten lifetimes to earn. And a man who, according to the evidence, siphoned millions from company accounts for his own use."

I let the pause breathe.

"You will hear testimony from Ms. Vesper, who saw the fraud firsthand. You will see documents—emails, bank records—that connect Mr. Lyle directly to the embezzlement. You will hear how, when Ms. Vesper refused to stay quiet, Mr. Lyle retaliated. How he used his position to intimidate her, harass her, make her life a living hell. You'll hear how Mr. Lyle tried to buy her silence for a quarter of a million dollars and…"

I trailed off. I was the first person to realize my

mistake. I shut my mouth and tried to swallow down the words I'd just said. They didn't retreat.

I was facing the judge's bench, the words in the air between us. Theo's brow lifted. Just the slightest arch, but enough to tell me—oh, hell. He knew. He knew what I'd just done.

Across the counsel table, Amira's and Jackson's eyes went wide, twin spotlights of *What the hell just happened?* They knew too.

The silence spread out between us like a slick on water. Heavy. Waiting.

Archibald, of course, was the last to catch up. I could almost hear the hamster wheel squeaking in his head. Then, like a kid realizing the teacher had left the classroom and the test was unguarded, he straightened in his chair.

"Objection, Your Honor!"

His voice was triumphant but late. So late it was almost pathetic.

I didn't look at him. I kept my eyes on Theo, who was watching me with the same steady calm as if he were deciding whether to pull me out of the hole I'd just dug…or hand me the shovel.

The heat crawled up my neck, but my face stayed stone. "Withdrawn," I said evenly, even though the words tasted like defeat. Inside, I was cursing myself six ways to Sunday. Because I knew exactly what I'd just done.

Settlement talks. I'd put the number right out there like I was reading it off a diner menu. Rookie mistake. Rule one in litigation: you don't talk about settlements. Not in opening, not in testimony, not if someone held a gun to your head. Settlement discussions are confidential, protected, inadmissible. It's in the damn rules—federal, state, take your pick.

Why? Because the law likes to pretend that people can try to resolve things without a jury—or in this case, a judge—thinking it's some kind of admission of guilt. Mentioning it makes you look like you're trying to bias the court with a dollar sign, and judges hate that. Especially judges with a stickler streak.

Like this judge clearly did. Theo had been given more than one out to not recuse himself. He hadn't taken any of the offerings until I agreed. He'd still thought me ethical. Until that slip.

I saw it in that raised brow. There was no judgment, just sharp awareness, like he could still taste my mistake in the air. It was small enough that I could recover but big enough that I knew he'd seen me at less than my best. And I hated that.

I never made errors. Not in court. Not where it

mattered. And now, on the one day I needed to be razor sharp in front, I'd just given the defense a gift-wrapped detail to hammer later.

But I didn't stop. I couldn't stop.

"Mr. Lyle tried to make Ms. Vesper's life a living hell. But she didn't back down. And by the end of this trial, you will see why her truth matters—and why the law is on her side."

I returned to my seat, keeping my face neutral, like nothing had gone wrong. But inside, my confidence had taken a hit. Not because Archibald had seen it. Not because my juniors had seen it.

Because the judge had.

CHAPTER ELEVEN

By the time I pulled into the driveway, I'd replayed that slip-up in court so many times I could've filed it as Exhibit A in my own incompetence. Sure, I'd recovered. Gotten back into rhythm. Made my points. But it didn't matter. I'd wanted Theo to see me at my best. Instead, I'd handed him a rookie mistake in the first few minutes.

First impressions, right?

Though that hadn't been his first impression of me. He'd liked what he'd seen of me as a woman twice before this morning's debacle. Last night in that hotel room made that clear enough. But that had been date-me. I spent the least of my time in that role. I was a prosecutor for the other ninety percent of my life. And that's all he'd ever see me as from this day forward.

We'd never be in a hotel room again. Never at a bar, flirting. Never feed that spark between us into a crackling fire. That door had slammed shut before it even had the chance to open all the way.

I suddenly had a craving for coffee. The real kind, hot and black, even though it was past seven in the evening and I'd regret it when I was wide awake around two a.m.

I got out of the car and nearly ran into a young woman trying to sneak out of my basement door. She froze like I'd caught her shoplifting. Then she had the audacity to wave with an embarrassed smile.

"Hey, Ms. Lana."

It took me a second to place her. Mostly because the last time I'd seen her she'd been wearing braces and a prom dress. Hannah Cooper? Daughter of Dave and Linda Cooper. She'd been friends with Brittany in high school.

She was in her twenties now, which was old enough to know better. But then, so was my ex. Not in his twenties, of course. But he was old enough to know better than to date a woman his own daughter's age. I was sure he didn't feel the slightest twinge of guilt about sneaking around with a girl young enough to be his daughter. And yet no one was going to make him recuse himself from that relationship.

Hannah ducked her head like a kid caught stealing cookies and scurried toward the street. I watched her ponytail swish as she all but speed-walked away, legs pumping, heels clicking too fast on the cracked pavement. She didn't even look back. Not once. Not at me. Not at the house she'd just slunk out of like it was a cheap motel. Just kept going, shoulders hunched until she rounded the corner and was gone.

I stood there a beat longer, disbelief sour on my tongue, disgust simmering in my gut. I didn't want to go inside my house. But this was where I lived.

Inside, my mother was at the stove, stirring a pot like the kitchen was her stage and she'd been playing this role all her life. My granddaughter giggled as she sat on the counter, grabbing for a wooden spoon twice her size.

In the corner, Brittany had her back to us, voice low but cracking on the phone with her husband. "When are you coming home?" she asked, tears barely held back. There was a pause, then, softer still, "I know, but... the account's overdrawn again." Another pause. "No, I'm not blaming you. I just... I'll take care of it, okay? Fine. I love you..."

She jerked, then pulled the phone away from her ear and stared at the device like she was looking at it for the first time.

"I think you might be right, Grandma." Emily's phone was in her lap, her eyes actually connecting with her grandmother.

"What did I say about the G word, Emily?"

"I think I'm going to stop looking for a job and find a man instead, GG."

"In my day, that's what success looked like —a ring on your finger."

"Being a feminist certainly isn't paying off. My last job fired me because I called in sick. But I swear, someone in the interview had a bug, and they coughed right on me. And then I took a mental health day the next week. And yeah, okay, I asked to leave early when Taylor dropped her surprise album, but that's not a reason to fire somebody."

Evaline nodded like she was listening to the testimony of a wronged saint.

I looked at my daughters. Really looked. Had all those years of stepping in, fixing everything, carrying everyone… handicapped them? I'd let them take "mental health days" from school when they weren't feeling up to it. It hadn't seemed like a big deal at the time—just school. English and math. It wasn't life.

But me? I'd never once taken a sick day at work. Well, not outside of pregnancy, and even then, I hadn't taken all of my maternity leave. I'd limped into work swollen, exhausted, and stitched back together because things had to get done. I'd raised my girls on speeches about equal rights and equal pay. So why were they still falling short?

Myles came up the stairs, smelling like my bath soap. He was freshly showered, but the evidence was all over him—flushed skin, that lazy, loose gait he only had after sex. I knew the signs. I'd been married to the man long enough to read him like a bad novel I kept hoping would get better.

I looked at him. Really looked. Once upon a time, he'd been a go-getter. Back when we first got together, he was knee deep in starting his own business. He'd just graduated from college with a degree in software engineering, but decided to follow his bliss as a chef. He'd started a food truck, a gourmet hot dog stand that only sold toppings named after famous philosophers. "The Nietzsche" was a bratwurst with extra sauerkraut. It hadn't been immediately successful. It probably wouldn't have been in a city full of people who thought ketchup counted as an exotic condiment.

Meanwhile, my career was taking off. Had I suggested he stay at home with Brittany? Or had he brought it up? I honestly couldn't remember. The years blurred together into one long stretch of me bringing home the health insurance and him "working on ideas."

Had I emasculated him? Had I handicapped him the way I'd apparently done with the girls? Running a hand through his shampooed hair, Myles smiled at me like nothing in the world could touch him. And why would it? I was still taking care of him.

"Hey, Lanabanana," he said, easy as you please.

I didn't bother with small talk. "We've been over this, Myles. Twice now in one week. No girls in my basement."

Myles huffed—actually huffed—like I'd just reminded him to take out the trash instead of called him out on breaking the one boundary I had left with him. "You need to get some, Lana," he said, like it was helpful advice. "If you want, you can come slink into the basement. The offer of exes with bene-fits is always on the table."

Then he walked past me and disappeared into the kitchen, where he was greeted like a hero returning from war. No one looked at me. Not my daughters, not my mother, not the grandbaby giggling in her high chair. They carried on like I wasn't there. Like I was just part of the furniture—reliable, unremarkable, easy to ignore.

I slipped down the hall to my bedroom and immediately banged my toe against one of Chloe's overflowing storage bins. The sharp edge caught me right on the bone. I hissed through my teeth, clutching the doorframe like I'd just been shot.

My middle child was halfway around the world chasing sunsets and selfies, but her junk was still colonizing my house like kudzu. I bit back a curse, limped the rest of the way, and told myself I wasn't going to cry over a damn toe—or the fact that even in my own hallway, I couldn't walk two steps without tripping over someone else's baggage.

Once inside my bedroom, I shut the door and pulled out my phone. Myles was right. I did need to get some. Staring down at the dating app I'd downloaded in a moment of wine-fueled optimism, I came to the quick realization that I didn't want to see any of those men. I didn't want clever bios or filtered smiles. I wanted that hotel bar. I wanted to lean against the counter, feel the low thrum of music in my chest, and talk to Theo like we had no idea who the other person was.

But that wasn't going to happen ever again.

I tossed the phone on the bed and pulled out my trial notes instead. If I couldn't talk to Theo, I could at least stand in front of him tomorrow and be flawless. He was going to see me at my best—razor-sharp, unshakable, impossible to ignore.

CHAPTER TWELVE

Tessa opened the door, gave me a slow once-over, and smirked. "Well, well. You're wearing your boss bitch suit."

She wasn't wrong. It was the navy pantsuit I'd had custom-made in New York. The outfit was tailored to my body in lines so sharp it could slice bread. The jacket nipped in at the waist, the trousers skimmed just enough to hint there were actual legs under there, and the silk blouse underneath was the color of fresh bruises—deep plum, almost black. Not an off-the-rack stitch in sight. This was the kind of outfit that made opposing counsel check their notes twice and wait staff call me miss instead of ma'am.

It was also murderously uncomfortable, but that was beside the point.

I brushed past Tessa into her house. "And you, my dear friend, are about to make this boss dangerous. Do my makeup?"

Tessa fell into step behind me toward the bathroom. "What's going on?"

"Let's wait until Celia gets here with the coffee before I explain," I said, unbuttoning my coat. "You know how she gets if she thinks we've been talking without her."

Celia was still stuck in high school girl mode—never quite believing she was part of the clique. Tessa and I had been friends first, the way Bo and Celia had been friends first. The difference was that Tessa and I had pulled Celia into our girl gang without hesitation. Celia had never done that with her and Bo's friendship for us. Now all these years later, Celia still carried herself like she needed a visitor's pass when she hung with me and Tessa.

Tessa flicked on the bathroom light. Her counter was already a war zone of palettes, brushes, and tubes. She carried in a barstool and placed it in front of the mirror. I sat.

She stood behind me, arms folded. "What's the vibe here? Smoky and dangerous? Soft and approachable? Courtroom, but make it couture?"

I met her eyes in the mirror. "I'm going for make-him-regret."

Her brow lifted, approval arching the perfectly plucked hairs there. Then she grinned like a cat with fresh cream. "Say no more."

And she didn't. She just started working, leaning in close, the bristles of her brush whispering across my skin. Tessa didn't ask who he was or why he needed to regret anything.

Her arsenal was spread across the counter—an organized chaos of palettes, tubes, and compacts, each one like a little jewel box. Golds, bronzes, rich berry reds, deep cocoa browns—colors that sang against her honey-golden skin. Tessa's parents were from the Caribbean islands. She wore that heritage like sunlight had decided to move in permanently. I tanned well enough, thanks to my Italian heritage, but after two generations here, my skin didn't hold the same molten warmth hers did. Still, her colors worked on me. She knew exactly which shades would sharpen my cheekbones, make my eyes sharper, my mouth less resting bitch and more seductively dangerous.

Perched on the stool in front of the mirror, I watched while she wielded a brush like she was about to paint the Sistine Chapel on my face. She hummed along to some slow, breathy yoga studio playlist in the background. I sat still, resisting the urge to check my phone.

I watched her work in the mirror for a while, her brows slightly drawn in concentration, her bracelets clinking softly every time she dipped into a palette. Then, before I could talk myself out of it, I asked, "Do you think I'm too much?"

"I think you're the perfect amount."

"I'm serious."

"So am I."

I lifted one shoulder, careful not to mess up whatever she was doing around my jawline. "I mean… am I one of *those* women?"

"One of what women?"

"You know. A too-much-woman." I made a vague, sweeping gesture toward my reflection. "Too much for a man. Too much to have girlfriends. The kind of woman people say they admire but don't actually want to deal with."

Tessa gave a low hum, the kind that was meant to be noncommittal but carried an opinion all the same.

"I'm not fishing for a compliment. I just… I mean, look at me and Celia. We practically broke up for decades because I overreacted."

I saw it—the slight tightening at the corners of Tessa's mouth. She didn't disagree.

"Exactly," I muttered.

Tessa set down the brush and picked up another one, softer, fluffier. "Real talk, babe? Myles should have risen to the occasion." Her tone was that gentle, yoga-instructor calm that somehow made me feel like I'd been both comforted and scolded. "And you and Celia are repairing your friendship. Things take time."

"That's adorable. You should knit that on a pillow."

Tessa ignored me. "The right man will come along. Look how long it took Bo and Celia."

"Mm." My non-answer said plenty.

Tessa paused, tilting her head to study my face like she was making sure my eyeliner was even—or maybe deciding if I was worth arguing with. Then, without warning, she stopped completely, brush in midair.

"Is this about your one-night stand?"

I didn't answer.

"Ha! I knew it." She rolled her eyes and went back to brushing some impossibly fine powder across my cheekbones. "Lana Russo, you are impossible."

"No, I'm too much," I corrected. "We've established that."

The thing was, I wasn't entirely joking. The thought had been gnawing at me all week, in the spaces between work and the noise of my family. I'd been told my whole life I was "a lot." In school, it was "bossy." In my marriage, it was "nagging." In court, it was "intimidating." And every time, I'd worn it like armor, because what was the alternative—shrinking?

But the older I got, the heavier the armor felt. And sometimes I wondered if I'd been so busy proving I didn't need anyone that I'd made sure I didn't have anyone.

Tessa didn't rush to fill the silence. She never did. That was one of the things I liked about her; she didn't need to hear herself talk.

Finally, she said, "You know what I think?"

"This is the part where you tell me to open my third eye and eat more leafy greens?"

"I think," she began, ignoring me again, "that the man from your one-night stand has you questioning yourself. Not because you're doubting yourself but because you're doubting who everyone else thinks you are. And that's not necessarily a bad thing. But don't mistake questioning for doubting."

I sat back slightly, studying her in the mirror.

"That's… surprisingly deep for someone who once told me her dog was her soul mate."

"Hey, Yoda was the best dog in the world. He's looking down at me from doggie heaven."

I smirked but didn't push it. The truth was, she wasn't wrong. Theo had managed to look at me like he saw everything and still wanted it. Not the polished courtroom version, not the mom-who-keeps-it-all-running version. Just… me. If there was a surer way to feel like too much and not enough all at once, I hadn't found it yet.

Tessa finished with the blush and stepped back. "There. Make him regret."

I turned toward the mirror and saw her work. Sharp lines. Strong eyes. Lips that could win arguments without ever speaking.

"Perfect," I said, and even managed to keep my voice steady.

But as she packed away the brushes, I kept my eyes on my reflection, wondering who exactly I was getting all dressed up for—and whether he was worth the trouble.

The front door opened, and the smell of hot coffee came barreling down the hall ahead of Celia. She stepped into the bathroom doorway, paper cups in hand, her eyes sweeping over me. One eyebrow arched.

"Well, well," she said, a slow grin tugging at her mouth. "Who is this boss bitch about to make regret their life choices?"

I cracked first, laughter spilling out of me before I could stop it. Tessa followed, the sound warm and easy.

Celia's grin faltered just enough for me to see it— the flicker of that left-out look she'd never quite been able to shake, like she was waiting for us to remember she wasn't in on the joke.

I held out my arms. "You know me so well," I said.

The look broke, and she stepped in, coffee first.

CHAPTER THIRTEEN

The marble steps outside the courthouse were slick from last night's rain, but I didn't break stride. If I was going down, it wasn't going to be because of a puddle. My heels clicked against the stone like a metronome, sharp and steady, announcing me before I even made it through the doors.

"Lana Russo," a voice called, as bright and piercing as the church bell on Sunday mornings.

I didn't have to turn to know who it was. Mrs. Thelma Denton—Stillwater Springs' self-appointed town crier—was perched on the bench out front, pearls knotted around her throat, umbrella in hand like a scepter.

"Well, would you look at you," she said, giving me

a once-over so thorough I almost expected her to demand I twirl. "That suit's sharp enough to slice a man in two. It's not just any suit—that's a notice me suit if ever I saw one."

"It's a work suit." I adjusted the strap of my briefcase and tried to move around her.

No such luck. She stood in my path. Unfortunately, my mother had raised me with enough manners to not knock down an elderly woman.

"Nonsense. A woman doesn't wear heels that high unless she's out to remind someone she's still got legs worth looking at. You dating again? Heard Myles is keeping himself busy."

Of course she'd bring up Myles. The whole town knew he'd been cheating on me while we were married and sleeping with anything with a pulse after. They always said it with pity, though. Pity that clung to me like static, as if I were the one to be ashamed. At least Ms. Thelma's tone was tinged with disgust. But I wasn't about to spill my tea with her. Not unless I wanted it discussed over tea time at the next Bingo night.

"No dates, Ms. T. Just a job to do."

Her eyes narrowed like she didn't believe a word of it, but she smiled all the same. "Well, whoever's on the other side of that courtroom better be worried. You look like trouble in heels."

"Thanks, Ms. T."

I gave her a tight smile and pushed the courthouse doors open. My pulse thrummed harder than it should've. I was here to do my job. I always did. But I'd be lying if I said I didn't want Theo Marsden to look up from the bench and notice. Not just the suit. Not just the heels. Me.

The boss bitch suit was earning its keep this morning. I could've gone with black, but it hides too much. Charcoal makes people work to read you. And right now, I wanted them trying to figure me out.

My makeup was bulletproof, thanks to Tessa. With every contour in place, every line precise enough to cut glass. I'd been in court long enough to know it wasn't about vanity—it was strategy. You want people listening to your words, but it never hurts when they can't look away from your face.

The security guard at the metal detector gave me a nod that was half respect, half appreciation. Inside, the air was already buzzing. Lawyers conferring in corners, clerks shuffling papers, the scent of burnt coffee lingering like an unwelcome witness.

I had my game face on. This was my arena. My

case to win. My day to put yesterday's mistake behind me.

And then I saw him.

Theo.

It was like someone pulled the emergency brake on my morning. He was standing at the far end of the lobby, just past the elevators, with a woman I didn't know. She was tall and sleek, dressed like she'd been born in a country club and raised on the belief that she'd never have to iron her own clothes. The two of them were smiling, their heads bent toward each other. The low hum of their laughter drifted toward me over the din of the courthouse.

Her hand landed on his arm. Not a friendly tap. Not a fleeting brush. The kind of touch that implied she was welcome there. That she'd been there before.

Theo glanced down at her hand like he was weighing its meaning. Then—God help me—he sighed. Not annoyed. Not flattered. Was that regret?

What the hell did that mean? Was he regretting that he wouldn't be able to pursue something with her? Or that he already had?

Before I could decide if I wanted to know, his head lifted, and his eyes found me.

Regret melted off his face like it had never been

there. His expression lit up—quick, unguarded. A smile tugged at his mouth. The kind of smile a man couldn't fake. The kind of smile that came when you were standing in a crowd of acquaintances and then you saw someone you actually wanted to see.

And then, God help me, I lit up too. From the inside out, I felt myself stretching. I stood up higher on my tippy toes in my heels. My chest rose as I inhaled. And my lips tugged apart as I grinned back at him.

For a second, it was just us. No courthouse, no case, no recusal forcing us apart.

Just as quickly, the moment shuttered. Theo's smile eased back into something neutral, professional. I mirrored him. Lights out. Masks on.

I stepped forward, moving past the little tableaux of Theo and Club Monaco Barbie. My heels resumed their sharp, steady rhythm. I wasn't going to slow down, and I sure as hell wasn't going to stop.

I caught snippets of other people's conversations as I passed—motions to file, witnesses to wrangle, lunch orders to place. I gave a curt nod to a clerk I knew and kept walking. My heart was doing a drum solo in my chest, but no one needed to know that.

The courtroom doors were ahead, heavy oak with brass handles worn down by decades of sweaty palms. I pushed them open like I owned the place because in my mind, I did. Inside, the hum quieted just enough to notice me.

I took my seat at the prosecution's table, set my briefcase down, and pulled out my files. My hands were steady. My pulse was not.

It wasn't that I wanted Theo to want me. It was that I wanted him to see me but only at my best. I wanted him to see me today, sharp and in control. And fine, I didn't want him to see anyone else in the meantime.

I was going to win this case. I was going to do it in front of him. And if he walked away from this courthouse without thinking about what it might be like to have me in his corner—in court or other rooms—then I'd clearly lost my touch.

A shadow passed in my peripheral vision. I didn't have to look to know it was him entering the court-room. His presence came with a booming announcement. I rose, but I didn't turn my head. I didn't give him the satisfaction.

The air shifted, the way it does when a storm moves in—not yet raining but promising it. I slid a pen across my legal pad like I was loading ammuni-tion into my weapon. My armor was in place. My game face was locked on.

By mid-morning, the whistleblower case was mine. Every document I introduced slid into evidence without so much as a scratch. Every question I asked landed exactly where I wanted it to. Every time Archibald tried to rattle Claire Vesper or one of my experts, I was up on my feet before his words had finished echoing.

"Objection. Argumentative."

Sustained.

"Objection. Misstates the witness's prior testimony."

Sustained again.

After the third one, Archibald shot me a look like a gambler watching his last chip slide to the other side of the table. I didn't smile. But others in the courtroom did. The defense table was already counting their losses.

Claire held firm on the stand. Calm. Direct. Not once looking at Richard Lyle, the man who had been her boss, the man who'd spent a quarter-million dollars trying to shut her up.

Amira and Jackson sat to my left, notes at the ready, wearing matching little half-smirks like they'd just spotted blood in the water.

Theo… well, Theo wore that judicial mask like it had been carved for him. Elbows on the bench, fingers steepled, gaze steady. But I'd seen his ecstasy face in that hotel room. I knew the difference between neutral and biting back a reaction. He knew I was winning.

When Archibald tried to get Claire to admit she had "misinterpreted" an internal email chain, Theo's gaze flicked to me expectantly just as I shifted my weight to my feet to stand. I cut Archie off before Claire even took a breath.

"Objection. The document speaks for itself."

"Sustained," Theo said without missing a beat. As though we were completely in tune. "Move on, Mr. Stalworth."

It was going so smoothly I could almost have forgotten about yesterday's disaster—almost.

I ran Claire through the last few pieces of evidence: the unsigned checks, the bank transfer logs, the conveniently timed accounting adjustments. Each answer fit neatly into the narrative I'd built. And each time, I caught Theo jotting something in his notes. Not much, just a single line here and there, but I knew exactly what that meant—he was tracking my points.

"Your Honor," I said when Claire stepped down, "the prosecution rests."

It wasn't theater. I didn't need theater. The

evidence spoke loud enough without me waving my arms around. Still, I let the words hang in the air for a moment, just long enough for the tension to register at the defense table.

"Thank you, Ms. Russo." Theo's voice was steady, giving nothing away. "We'll adjourn for the day and reconvene tomorrow at nine sharp. Counsel, be prepared to proceed without delay."

I gathered my notes but not before I caught Theo's gaze again. Just for a second. No smile. No wink. Just that steady, unreadable judge face.

Except I'd seen the flicker there, the one he thought he'd hid well. The one that told me he knew I'd just walked him through a winning case.

CHAPTER FOURTEEN

I slid behind the wheel, still humming with the aftertaste of victory. Not the champagne kind. More like a slow-burn buzz that vibrated under the skin, a reminder that I could still walk into a courtroom and make it mine.

I'd been sharp today. Clean. Every objection sustained. Every point landed. Even Archibald's smug little half-smile had cracked around the edges by the end. So why was I sitting here in my car, staring at the dashboard like it might tell me what to do with myself?

I didn't want to go home. Home meant the basement ex-husband, the adult daughters who still acted like they needed permission slips from me, and my mother playing matriarch over a kitchen I paid for.

It meant stepping right back into the role I'd been playing for decades, the one I was too damn good at to ever get free from.

I didn't want to celebrate with Amira and Jackson either. I could already hear them cheering, "You killed it today" while ordering something with too much sugar and not enough alcohol, trying to drag me into selfies. No.

And the app? God. The app was an endless catalog of men who looked like they'd ask me to split the check and then "forget" their wallet. Or want me to change their bedpans.

My hands tightened on the steering wheel, my foot pressed down on the gas pedal. When had I started driving? Where exactly was I?

Wait, I knew this street. I knew that neon sign. I knew the faint pulse of jazz music coming through the walls. I'd parked outside that damn bar. The one where Theo had looked at me like I wasn't just a woman at the end of her rope but someone he wanted to reach for. The one where I'd let myself forget every rule I lived by.

I told myself I was just going in for a drink. He wouldn't be there. Of course he wouldn't. I'd have one glass of whiskey, maybe two, watch the world go by, then head home before I did anything truly stupid, like look him up. I had his last name now. He wouldn't be hard to find. Except I knew exactly where he'd be tomorrow. Sitting on a bench out of my reach.

There were plenty of other stupid things I could do. Not that there was anything stupid that I wanted to do. I didn't have a current lover. No ex-lover I wanted to go back to. Unless we were talking about the one I was barred from. So into the bar I went.

It was warm and dim inside. The air carried the tang of lime and bourbon. The faint perfume of someone's cologne drifted past. I didn't bother with a booth. I wasn't hungry. I slid onto a stool at the far end of the bar, ordered my drink, and settled into the rhythm of people-watching.

The door opened. My pulse jumped. A guy in a ball cap who looked like he'd get carded at a PG-13 movie. Not him.

It opened again. A woman in a sharp skirt suit, eyes glued to her phone. Not him.

The door kept opening and kept disappointing me. Every time it swung wide, I felt that flash—hope and dread knotted together—only to have it dissolve into nothing.

The bartender came back, wiping down the counter. "Another?"

I hesitated, weighing whether I wanted to nurse my buzz into the kind of warm, fuzzy edge that would let me sleep tonight without replaying the day on a loop.

"She'll take a coffee."

It was him.

Theo slid onto the stool two seats away from me. He looked… casual. Dangerous in a way that had nothing to do with the bench and everything to do with the fact that he'd once had his hands on me, his mouth on mine.

Steam curled up from the mug when it landed in front of me, like it had something to say. I didn't care what the beverage thought. I cared what it meant. Was this about making sure I sobered up? Like at the hotel, when he'd handed me coffee before…

The night at the hotel—his mouth hot against mine, his hands everywhere, his tongue exactly where I needed it. Was this the same move? Making sure I sobered up before we… what? Went for round two?

"When I was a kid, my dad decided to teach me how to fish."

I looked up to see Theo talking to the bartender. The man glanced at Theo as though to ask, *Are you talking to me?* Then he glanced at me, then at the two empty chairs between us.

Theo kept talking, his gaze on the bartender even after the man had topped his drink. "We didn't own a boat, so he 'borrowed' my uncle's canoe. But he didn't tell him. Dad forgot to check for leaks, so halfway across the lake…" Theo made a slow sinking motion with his hand. "We're bailing water with a bait bucket while my mother's on shore screaming that she told him so."

I blinked at Theo, unsure if this story was meant for me. Was this a cautionary tale? A lesson I was supposed to learn? Insider information about the case?

It had nothing to do with anything between us. There wasn't supposed to be anything between us. Not while the case was ongoing.

Theo kept talking. To the bartender, not to me. This wasn't his usual measured, judicial tone. His voice was looser, warmer, like we were sitting on some back porch instead of a sticky barstool.

"Let me tell you the story of how my parents met."

"Ohhh… kay," the bartender agreed. It wasn't like the bar was busy.

The place was nearly empty. A lone man hunched

over the counter three stools down, nursing a beer. His eyes were glued to the baseball game flickering across the mounted TV, the announcer's voice droning through the speakers like white noise.

In the far corner, a couple sat in a booth, bodies angled away from each other, their silence louder than the game on TV. The woman tapped her straw against the side of her glass, staring at the door like she was already calculating her escape. The man adjusted his tie over and over again. A date gone bad and not even late enough for either of them to pretend otherwise.

The only waitress in sight was slouched at a table near the back, her apron hanging loose as she thumbed through her phone, the blue glow lighting up her bored expression.

"They were on rival baseball teams," Theo said, his mouth quirking like the memory wasn't his but he'd been told it so many times it might as well be. "My dad was running for home; my mom was catching. She blocks the plate. He tries to slide—she claims she was going for the tag, but her elbow just happened to come up hard enough to rearrange his face. Instead of reading her the riot act, he asked her out. Bandages and all. Their first date was at a diner where he ordered soup because he couldn't chew.

She spent the whole meal making fun of how pathetic he looked."

Theo took a sip of his drink, eyes going a little distant before they warmed again. For a moment, he wasn't here at the bar; he was somewhere else entirely. Back in that dust cloud on a softball field. Or maybe in a beat-up car under a moon.

I wondered if his parents were still alive. Had he lost them? I didn't know. Truth was, I didn't know much of anything about him. I knew what he looked like in a hotel bed. I knew the sound he made when something felt too good for him to control his reactions. I knew his poker face in court. But this face? This expression? This was new to me.

I looked at him and wondered who he was when no one was watching. No one was watching. Just me. The bartender stood in front of him, a truly captive audience, but the man's gaze was on the glass tumbler he was polishing.

Theo didn't look at me. Not once. But I knew he was talking to me.

His eyes caught mine in the reflection of the mirror behind the bar. His gaze was lit, open. It didn't do that thing he'd done in the courthouse hallway this morning. No dimming. No dampening. He let me see him. In the reflection, I could swear I saw my own light growing, catching on something between us neither of us had the good sense to smother.

"What are you doing?" I asked. "Why are you telling me this?"

"I'm not talking to you. I'm talking to my new friend…?"

"Ansen," said the bartender.

"I'm just letting Ansen get to know me. Ansen and I aren't talking about our work. No case. Just me and him at the bar. For anyone else listening in, it's just hearsay."

My fingers curled around the warm ceramic cup. Then I pushed the coffee away like it was something toxic. "In that case, strike the coffee from the record, Ansen. I'm going to need something stronger if I'm going to sit through this trial."

Theo's laughter was a deep, bright thing. It lifted the weight that had been on my shoulders and left me feeling light and carefree. Ansen just looked between the two of us. Then he very deliberately set the tip jar between us.

CHAPTER FIFTEEN

I woke up with that slippery, honey-thick kind of guilt that doesn't make you sick —it makes you smile into the pillow. I hadn't spoken a single word to Theo. Well, not after I asked him what he was doing. After that, every syllable had been aimed at Ansen, the bartender, who now knew more about my childhood than half my family.

Theo and I had talked to him all night. Well— through him. Stories of scraped knees and teenage mistakes. Bad haircuts. First heartbreaks. Ansen got the direct eye contact, the questions, the punchlines, and a big tip. But Theo got my laugh, and I got his. It was ridiculous and juvenile and reckless.

Based on the pop culture references Theo tossed into his stories—movies he saw in theaters, songs he claimed as "his"—I had him pegged somewhere in his mid-thirties. I didn't ask. Couldn't. Wouldn't.

God, what if he was twenty-nine?

No. That wasn't plausible. Most states require judges to have been licensed attorneys for at least five years. If he'd graduated law school in his mid-twenties, he had to at least have crossed the thirty-year mark. Still. Thirty-anything looked different from this side of forty-nine.

It wasn't the math of it that bothered me. Ten years. Twelve, maybe. Men did it all the time, collected women half their age like they were trading in last season's wardrobe. Nobody batted an eye. But a woman creeping up on fifty with a man who still had all his hair, no gut, and a metabolism that could burn off a pizza at midnight? Suddenly, it was cougar territory. Tabloid headline stuff.

And underneath all that noise was the quieter truth: I wasn't sure I trusted it. I knew what it meant to be wanted by men my own age. Not that all the men my age had their stuff together. The nurse or purse epidemic ran through every age bracket.

But Theo? He didn't need me to mother him. He didn't want me for my bank account. He wanted me. Me.

But what if he woke up one day and realized he

wanted children and a woman who could still give him some? What if he looked across the breakfast table one morning and wanted someone who didn't have the map of her life written in laugh lines and crow's feet? What if I soaked the bed with a hot flash one night? Perimenopause was no joke and had forced me out of the bed to change my nightshirt more than once this year.

It was wild that the age gap thing bothered me more than the ethics. The fact that last night, I'd danced along the razor's edge of judicial optics, balancing on the thin wire between "technically fine" and "suspension-worthy." I had never walked that close to the line before. Not in the twenty-plus years of doing this job. But with him?

God help me, it felt good.

I took my time dressing that morning. Not another Boss Bitch suit. No sharp charcoal or severe pinstripes. Today was a softer wool blend, the kind of cut that hinted at a waist without advertising it. A blouse with a neckline that suggested things without committing to them. Less *I'm here to crush your case into dust,* more *seduce me later, I dare you.*

Because if all went the way I planned, today the Jennings Dynamics case would come to rest. If the wind was at my back, Theo Marsden would render his verdict before we all went home.

And then?

Then I was going to make a beeline for his chambers, shut the door behind me, and cross every single line they'd drawn between us. Not just step over them—obliterate them. Burn the rulebook. Rewrite it in the margin of his lower back with my fingernails.

I told myself it was the rush of winning that made me feel like this—light, sharp, wired. But I knew better. It wasn't the case. It was him.

I found my mother in the kitchen, packing Tupperware into a tote bag. The back door was propped open, her suitcase waiting against the screen.

"Going somewhere?" I asked, though the answer was obvious.

"Gerald's back. The other woman—" Her lip curled around the word, but it didn't stop her hands from moving briskly. "—She left him, of course. I knew it wouldn't last, and he'd come crawling back to me. Men get those… urges. He's gotten it out of his system. Now he's ready for me to come home."

She'd said it was a money issue, hadn't she? I

opened my mouth. Closed it again with a sigh so heavy it felt like it carried forty years in its lungs. We'd had this conversation before. Hell, I'd lived this conversation before. My whole childhood had been the sound of doors closing, of my father's shoes walking out and my mother pretending not to hear. Pretending not to see. Pretending that "temporary" was something you could hang your dignity on.

This time, though, the roles had shifted. My father was long gone, off chasing whatever skirt had caught his attention in Florida. And Evaline Russo, nearly seventy and still carting Tupperware and blind devotion, had redirected her affections on to some man twenty years her junior. A man who had already left her once for a tighter package and had now returned, belly empty, ready to be fed and fussed over again.

She wanted to be wanted, even if it meant being mother and meal ticket rolled into one. And she called that love.

I leaned against the counter, the edge biting into my palms. My throat burned with words I wouldn't say. What was the point? She'd made her choice. She'd always make this choice.

"If you had only done this with Myles, shown

him you mean business by threatening to walk away, then you two would still be together."

"Thanks for that glowing piece of advice, Mom."

She came over and patted me on my cheek. "It's not too late for you, sweetie. But you should do something about those roots."

I jerked from her touch and then held the door open for her. She left without another word, thank all that was holy. I let the door shut behind her but felt gutted all the same. Because I knew somewhere deep down, I was terrified of becoming her.

That was the rot under my skin every time I looked at Theo. Not his age, not the stares we'd get, not the "cougar" headlines whispered behind coffee cups. No. It was the fear that I was Evaline, chasing a younger man who'd eventually realize he wanted someone else. Someone less complicated. Less tired. Less… me.

I did grab some of the ziti from the fridge because, through all her faults, my mother was an excellent cook. With the Tupperware in one hand, I picked my way through the living room, avoiding the mess my middle child had left behind. Only to see my eldest curled up on the couch, her head bent awkwardly against the armrest, one hand touching her phone like she'd fallen asleep mid-text. Her shoes were still on.

I crouched beside her and touched her shoulder. "Hey."

Brittany startled awake, lips parting. "Jack?"

Not exactly the first name I wanted to hear. She blinked, swiping at the crust in her eyes like it might erase the truth she'd just spoken into the room.

"Oh, hey, Mom."

"Hey, baby."

"Jack didn't come home last night," she said finally, voice low. "Dad was watching Maddie, and I didn't want to go back home alone."

We both knew what it meant. We both knew how that story ended. Because it was the same one I'd lived with Myles for years. Same one my mom had lived. Same script, different actors.

Brittany tilted her chin up, that defiant little move I'd seen since she was two and refusing to eat green beans. Waiting for me to deliver the blow. To say the thing—*leave him*—that would start the avalanche she wasn't ready for.

Instead, I sat. Not beside her, not across from her, just close enough that she'd have to see I wasn't moving until she spoke.

"Aren't you supposed to be in court?"

"I've got time."

Brittany swallowed, glancing toward the window like maybe the answer was out there. Finally, she said, "I want to go to counseling."

I didn't say anything.

"I don't want to be like…" Her eyes flicked to mine, and I knew the word she was about to use. She changed it at the last second. "…my parents. I want to keep my family together."

My tongue pressed hard against the back of my teeth, holding back the bitter retort that wanted to claw its way out. The one that wanted to say—*And what did that get me, Brit?*

But I didn't. I stayed quiet. Let her fill the space. There was no bartender. No reason I had to recuse. My daughter and I were allowed to have a relationship. Maybe it was time I tried to reach out. And the first step would be to keep my opinions to myself.

Brittany took the silence as permission and kept going. Words spilled out of her like she'd been holding them in for too long. How she thought maybe it was her fault, maybe she hadn't been paying enough attention, maybe if she worked harder—at home, at herself—he'd stop looking somewhere else.

I kept my face still. My breathing steady. I let her

keep talking because it wasn't my job right now to fix it or fix her. I just had to listen. Just be present.

It was the most uncharacteristic thing I'd done in years. Not solving the problem. Not building the escape hatch. Just sitting there in the half-light, my daughter unraveling next to me and letting the thread run out all on its own.

CHAPTER SIXTEEN

Amira caught me in the hallway before court. She slowed just enough to give me a once-over, her eyes narrowing, like she was trying to figure out what was different.

"You look… " A beat later, her expression cracked. "I'm so sorry. I never comment on another professional woman's clothes. That was uncalled for."

"Relax, Amira. And thanks for the compliment." Even though she hadn't given me a verbal compliment. The look in her eyes had said enough.

Amira wasn't the only person who noticed. Archibald noticed too, but for entirely different reasons. He was leaning against the defense table when I walked in, grinning like a man who thought charm could be substituted for substance.

"We should get drinks after this," he said, as if we'd just wrapped up some collegial moot court exercise and not been trying to gut each other over the past couple of days.

I gave him a long look, the kind I reserve for witnesses who are about to hang themselves with their own testimony. "What are you, like thirty?"

"Just turned forty. I get that a lot, though, that I look younger than my age. I'm guessing you get it too."

How was this guy in my age bracket? He didn't look young, just acted it. I shook my head. It didn't wipe the smile off his face. Clearly, he thought I was saying no to the age thing. I was saying no to the date thing.

Archie was one of those men who probably still thought he was the most interesting person in any given room. He wasn't. Not by a long shot. And definitely not on my level. Archibald played defense the same way he probably dated—flashy opening moves, overconfident middle game, and no real strategy to close.

The only man in this courthouse who was even

remotely in my league was sitting on the bench. Theo. God, I hoped he was mid-thirties.

Forty would be perfect. Forty meant he'd been around long enough to get kicked in the teeth a few times but not so long that the bruises had faded into resignation. Old enough to know what he wanted, young enough to still go after it.

The bailiff called the court to order. I slid into my chair, shuffling papers I didn't need to shuffle just to keep my eyes from drifting up to the bench too soon. But like clockwork, my gaze betrayed me.

Theo looked the same as he always did—composed, impassive, with the faintest hint of something sharper in the set of his jaw. He didn't scan the gallery or the lawyers like he was searching for something. He didn't need to. He already knew exactly where I was. And I knew exactly where he was.

It wasn't visible. It wasn't audible. But there was a pull between us, like a fine wire stretched taut. Each day of this trial, the wire wound tighter. You could almost hear it hum if you listened hard enough.

I could hear my inner voice—the one that had kept me from wrecking my life more than once—telling me to get my head in the game, that nothing good could come from letting a man like Theo Marsden inside my defenses.

The thing about defenses? Sometimes you get tired of holding the line.

I sat there, taking in the faint shine of the wood paneling, the stale mix of old paper and floor polish in the air, and the sound of the bailiff's voice announcing the case. I kept my eyes forward. I didn't let myself look at Theo again.

But I felt him. Every second. Every breath. Like that wire between us had wrapped around my ribs and tightened with each beat of my heart.

Archie came out swinging, but it didn't take long for me to see he'd left his gloves at home. From the moment he called his first witness, it was like watching a man try to patch a sinking ship with Post-it notes. My cross poked holes so fast and so clean the whole thing was hemorrhaging credibility before we hit the second question. Archie tried to pivot, but every answer his witness gave seemed to hand me another knife. I didn't even have to work for it. It was like the defense had decided self-sabotage was their closing argument.

Up on the bench, Theo didn't move much. But I'd started to recognize the subtleties. The faint tightening at the corner of his mouth. The way his eyes flickered just once before he smoothed his expression. He winced—barely—but I saw it. No one else would've caught it. You had to have studied him. Watched him when he was trying not to react. Spent enough time looking at him that the absence of a reaction was its own tell.

Like the rest of us, he was watching a slow-motion implosion. And not the kind you can recover from.

Archie must've felt it too, though he tried to keep the act going. He shuffled papers like they might rearrange themselves into something persuasive if he made enough noise. He cracked a joke that landed so flat the court reporter didn't even smirk.

If there had been a jury, they would have been shifting in their seats by now, avoiding eye contact, already writing him off. But this wasn't for a jury. This was for Theo. Which made every flinch I caught from the bench that much worse for Archie.

By the third witness, Archie's voice had the desperate edge of a man who could hear the trap closing but didn't know how to stop it. I'd hand him a contradiction, and he'd grab it like a lifeline, not realizing it was the rope I'd use to hang his argument.

The last cross was the cleanest cut of all. One

question, one answer, and the defense's story didn't just spring another leak—it capsized.

There was a long pause afterward. Archie stood there, blinking at his notes like they might whisper a miracle if he stared hard enough. They didn't.

Finally, he exhaled, the fight bleeding out of him in one long sigh. "The defense rests," he said, voice low, almost swallowed by the hum of the ceiling fans.

I didn't smile. Not outwardly. Inside, I could feel the current shift. Because Theo had winced again. And this time, he didn't bother to hide it.

Thankfully, it was closing time. Archie went first. He stood, straightened his jacket like he was about to pull a rabbit out of it, and launched into his closing. I'll give him this; he had presence. Smooth voice. Easy smile. If someone hadn't sat through the actual trial, they might even believe he had a leg to stand on. He painted his client as a misunderstood victim of circumstance, peppering his speech with phrases like "reasonable doubt" and "unsubstantiated claims."

The problem was, I'd spent the last two days tearing those claims apart in front of everyone. You could almost hear the air hissing out of his argument. Still, he pressed on, pacing like a man who thought motion could make up for lack of substance.

When he sat down, there was a flicker in Theo's eyes. Polite acknowledgment, nothing more. Then it was my turn.

I rose slowly. No need to rush the kill. My heels clicked against the tile as I stepped to the center of the room.

"Your Honor," I began, my voice even and measured. "The defense wants you to believe this is about a lack of proof. That what you've heard over the past couple of days is a story without substance. But stories don't hold up under cross-examination. Lies do not survive the light. Every time we held the defense's case to the light, it crumbled.

"This case is not about smoke and mirrors. It's about evidence. Evidence that the defendant knew exactly what they were doing. Evidence that they acted deliberately. Evidence that has not been refuted, only sidestepped. The defense would have you look away. I'm asking you to keep your eyes on the truth."

I walked him back through the key points: the paper trail, the testimony, the contradictions that weren't just mistakes but patterns. Each fact like a stone laid carefully in place. Build the wall. Leave no door.

"And so," I finished, my voice dropping just

enough to pull every ear toward me, "the only conclusion this court can reach is that the defendant is guilty as charged. Justice demands it. The evidence proves it. And the truth, Your Honor, is right here in front of you."

I returned to my seat, not looking at Archie, not even looking at Theo—because I didn't need to. I'd already seen it in his face before. The tell. The recognition.

Theo leaned forward, his hands folded on the bench. "I will take this case under advisement," he said, voice steady. "I will review the evidence and issue my decision in the morning."

He rose, robes shifting with the movement, and left through the side door. It closed softly behind him, but the sound echoed in my chest.

I knew I'd won. I'd have to wait a day, but after that verdict was read tomorrow—after there was no longer a case between us—I planned to find in his favor on one more matter. The one where we had another night together.

And who knew? Maybe more.

CHAPTER SEVENTEEN

The Jubilee prep was chaos. Folding tables leaned half-assembled against the wall, streamers sagged like limp pasta, and the smell of hot glue from some ill-conceived craft station clung to the air. Everyone had a job. Almost no one was doing it.

Celia and Bo were supposed to be tying ribbons on the giveaway baskets. Instead, they were in the corner, tying themselves into knots. With his hand on her waist, her laugh muffled against his mouth. Like teenagers who thought the world couldn't see them. I tried not to look. Tried harder not to roll my eyes.

Bo's daughter, Belle, was at my elbow, clipboard in hand, rattling off something about floral arrangements. Roses? Lilies? Did we want the color scheme to lean autumnal or patriotic?

I nodded at the right intervals, the way you do when you're not listening. Because I wasn't. My head was still back in the courtroom.

The case had ended cleanly enough, but the silence afterward had left too much space for my mind to wander. To Theo. To that particular brand of gravity he had when he leaned forward, listening like every word was a stone placed in the balance.

Once the case was over, once he rendered his verdict, what then? Ethically, yes, we'd be clear to have a relationship. He'd no longer be "Your Honor" and I'd no longer be standing on the other side of the bench. But ethically wasn't the same as wisely. Did I want that? Did I want him?

And what if he didn't decide in my favor? That thought stopped me cold. I hadn't even considered it until now. I had proven my burden—twice over. The defense was a disaster. Archie had stumbled so often he practically tripped into his closing. Still. All it took was one technicality, one lapse, one word twisted sideways, and we could be looking at a mistrial.

Theo wasn't the kind of man to hide behind technicalities. He'd rule on the case, not his feelings. And he'd rule for me. I mean, for my case. It was iron tight. I wasn't sure how he'd rule personally, though.

"Lana?"

Belle's voice cut through, sharp enough to make me blink. I looked at her, realizing she'd been speaking for a while. My nodding had fooled no one. She was glaring at me, then flicking her eyes to her father, who was still kissing Celia.

"I really need someone to get to work around here," Belle said. Her tone was dry enough that I almost smiled. Almost. Poor kid had inherited her mother's taskmaster gene but not the clout to back it up. Not yet.

"I'm here," Zach's voice piped up from across the room. He stepped forward, hands already reaching for the box Belle had been hovering over.

Belle's expression softened, like a cloud passing from the sun. She smiled at him—quick, grateful, uncalculated. And Zach… oh, Zach. The boy tried to hide it, but he was too much like his mother, who was still over in the corner, letting her feelings for Belle's dad shine. Zach might as well have tattooed his feelings for his soon-to-be stepsister on his forehead. That look. That quiet, ridiculous, aching look.

Adoration.

Zach snuck glances at Belle the way a starving

man sneaks glances at bread in the window of a bakery, bread he can't afford. Belle didn't notice. Or pretended not to. Hard to say with this generation. Either way, she stayed focused on her task, giving Zach instructions. He followed like a man with a compass that only pointed one way.

Two women drifted past the edge of my vision. They laughed about something private until their eyes met mine. The sound died in their throats when our gazes connected. Their faces rearranged themselves into masks of guilt, or shame, or maybe just annoyance that I'd noticed them at all.

Tiffany and Marcy. That's what their names were. Tiffany was the younger one, still in her twenties, always dressed like she was headed to some endless college mixer even though she'd dropped out years ago. I remembered her perfume more than her face, sharp and sugary, lingering in my basement after she left. She'd only been down there a couple of times that I knew of—but once was enough.

Marcy was the other. Thirties. Married. Pregnant now, her hand resting low on the curve of her stomach like she thought it made her look maternal instead of guilty. For one blink of a second, I wondered if the baby might've been Myles'. But then I reminded myself she was too far along; the timeline didn't match. No, her basement days were years behind her. I'd caught her sneaking out once, heels dangling from her hand, cheeks flushed. I'd just come home from court, fresh off a win that had cost me blood and bone, still humming with the sharpness of victory. And there she was, slipping out my side door like some tawdry cliché from a bad TV drama.

Two women, both fully aware of each other, both sharing the same community dick. And yet, here they were, still friends. Still giggling like teenagers. Until they saw me.

How did that work? Didn't girl code mean anything? I couldn't imagine sharing a man like that.

Celia had been in love with Bo her whole life, and even when they'd both married other people, the line between them never blurred into betrayal. It wasn't about sneaking around. It was about longing, about bad timing, about the kind of love you couldn't smother no matter how life tried to bury it.

Tessa and her husband? They'd been inseparable from their first date until his last breath. Theirs was a love story that made other people's marriages look like polite business arrangements.

But Myles? Myles had never inspired loyalty. In me, yes. I never cheated on him. Never considered it.

But when it came to other women, they used him. He was just heat and opportunity.

Women didn't love him. They consumed him. Passed him around like an appetizer. And he let them. I'd been the fool who had tried to turn him into a main course.

None of my girlfriends would've touched Myles with a ten-foot pole. Not Celia, not Tessa. They never even liked him. But me? I'd spent years defending him, smoothing the edges, making him look good. And in return, I got Tiffany and Marcy slipping in and out of my basement while I worked myself into the ground.

Looking at me now, laughter gone and mirth gone flat, Tiffany's lips pressed into a thin line. Marcy's hand went instinctively to her stomach, like I might accuse the baby. They turned, quick as a pair of startled deer, and headed the other way without a word.

The weight of the encounter lingered, pressing on my chest. All those years of being the one people pitied. Not him—never him. Myles went free, untouched, while I got the tilted heads, the whispered condolences, the unspoken accusation that I hadn't been enough.

What would people think if they saw me with

Theo? The first thing they'd say wouldn't be about ethics. It'd be about age. It'd be about how I was too old and he was too young. How I was desperate, and he was just using me or biding his time until something better, shinier came along.

Well, at least one thing I knew for certain: Whatever happened or didn't happen between me and Judge Marsden, I wouldn't have to fight my girlfriends over him.

"Theodore? Is that you?"

Tessa's voice, bright and lilting, carried across the hall. My eyes snapped up. And there he was, Theo, standing in the doorway of the Town Hall.

CHAPTER EIGHTEEN

He stood in the doorway, sunlight at his back, like some kind of golden idol sculpted by the gods just to torment me. Theo Marsden. The sight of him did something to my insides I had no business allowing. My pulse kicked up before I could stop it. Not like I had any control. My emotions, my organs, my thoughts all did what they wanted whenever he was around.

Handsome didn't even cover it. Theo looked edible. He smelled edible too. Though maybe that was my brain filling in blanks, conjuring up my favorite order from Wong's—fried rice drowned in soy sauce, egg rolls slick with oil, the hint of salt and garlic that clung to my fingers no matter how many napkins I used. That was Theo. A craving I'd had for dinner and wanted again warmed up in the morning until there was nothing left over.

My tongue darted out, a traitorous flick against my lips. And damned if his eyes didn't track the movement. His gaze was sharp and hungry, like he was starving and I was the buffet.

Suddenly there was movement. Arms wrapped around him, all that broad strength swallowed up by someone else's embrace. Tessa.

My best friend. My peaceful, granola-loving, namaste-chanting best friend. She was hugging Theo like he'd just returned from war. She was smiling up at him like the sun rose from his perfectly squared jaw.

And Theo? He grinned down at her. That grin I'd been hoarding in memory, rationing like contraband, and he just tossed it out to her like spare change.

I saw red. Real red. Not the subtle shade of irritation I lived in most days. The hot, violent flash of it. The kind of red that had me imagining snapping my best friend in two like she was one of her own organic breadsticks. God help me, the thought was fast and vicious.

I shook my head. No. Absolutely not. I was not

that girl. I wasn't that woman. And over a man, no less.

Tessa finally pulled away, her hands lingering like she had every right. She patted his cheek—patted it, like he was some golden retriever—and my molars nearly cracked.

"Theodore," she crooned, her voice thick with delight. "I can't believe how grown up you are."

Theodore.

My stomach dropped. Grown up? With Tessa's next words, the axe fell.

"I used to babysit him," she said, turning toward me, beaming like this was the most adorable revelation.

I gulped. The lump went down hard enough it hurt. My brain reeled, throwing up every case I'd ever argued, every closing statement, every sharp cross-examination. None of it had prepared me for this.

I'd slept with a man young enough for my best friend to have babysat. Babysat. As in diapers. As in cutting the crusts off sandwiches and singing lullabies.

Theo winced. Just a little twist of his mouth. I might have missed it if I didn't know the angles of his face by heart. But I did. He sighed, a long exhale, as if he already knew what was flashing through my mind: *He's too young for me.*

And the worst part? He didn't argue it. He couldn't. We weren't supposed to know each other.

Tessa clasped her hands together like she was about to start playing Patty Cake. "What are you doing in town?"

Theo flicked his eyes toward me—quick, guilty, like I was holding the answer on my tongue. "Filling in for a colleague." Vague. Non-committal. The kind of answer I'd shredded a hundred times in court.

Tessa's face lit up like she'd solved a riddle. "That's right—you're a lawyer, aren't you? How funny is that? Lana's a lawyer too."

Theo nodded at me. One clean dip of his chin, eyes skimming over me just long enough to sting.

I gave Tessa a weak smile. She didn't notice.

"We should all grab dinner together," she chirped. "We're just about done here."

Theo lifted a white paper bag. The smell hit me before the words did. "I just wrapped up a case," he said, casual, though his eyes never left mine. "Thought I'd treat myself to my favorite."

"Wong's? That's Lana's favorite restaurant. And it smells like—" Tessa squinted at the bag. "Wait. Is that fried rice and egg rolls?"

Theo nodded.

"That's Lana's favorite dish. What are the odds?"

Heat crawled up my neck. Odds. Sure. Nothing suspicious about the universe tossing me my exact craving in the hands of the man I wasn't supposed to want.

Theo's eyes flicked to mine again, sharp and knowing. A second too long. Enough for Tessa to catch it.

Her head swiveled between us. The air shifted.

"Well. I should get back to my hotel before this gets cold. Good seeing you again, Tessa."

"Likewise, Theodore."

We both watched him walk away. Broad shoulders, easy stride, sunlight catching the back of his hair. Tessa's head turned slowly. Her smile sharpened into something else. She jabbed a finger at me.

"Start talking."

For once, I didn't have an opening statement ready. My brain did the math—how much to admit, how much to bury. Luckily, salvation came in the form of Celia, who bounced up like she'd caught the scent of gossip on the wind.

"What'd I miss?"

"Just that Lana's booty call showed up, and apparently our BFF is a cougar."

Celia's brows shot up. "Who?"

Before Tessa could sing it from the rooftops, I hissed and shoved them both into the corner. The same corner where Celia had been tangled up with Bo not ten minutes ago. Great. Romance Alley.

I lowered my voice. "He's the judge on the case I've been prosecuting. We didn't know it at the time."

"Oh?" sighed Celia. "So what does that mean? Can you date him after the case?"

I didn't bother answering because the truth sounded messy even in my own head.

Tessa wasn't letting me off the hook. "Do you even want to date him? Because I know for a fact Theodore is a great guy."

"He's a kid," I snapped.

"Please," Tessa scoffed. "He's only—"

I cut her off with a shush and a wave of my hand. I didn't want to know. I didn't want any confirmation of his age.

"He was always mature for his age. He comes from a great family. He's never been in trouble. He's very respectful. I barely had to watch him when I babysat him. He cleaned up after me. He's the whole package."

Oh, and what a package. If only she knew. If either of them knew what he and I had gotten down to in that hotel room, "respectful" wouldn't exactly make the list of adjectives to describe Theodore Marsden.

But Tessa and Celia knew me too well. That thought must've slipped across my face, because both of their eyes narrowed on me.

"I've never seen you react to someone like this, babe," said Tessa. "Don't let age stand in your way."

Age wasn't the only problem. At least not for now. The case was. So I kept my mouth shut, while their eyes kept digging for answers I wasn't ready to hand over.

Movement caught my eye across the street. My son-in-law—Mr. Perfect Husband, Mr. Family Man —was slinking into a side building like a teenager sneaking back on prom night after curfew. Not alone either. A woman followed, quickly, head ducked, heels clicking too fast against the sidewalk.

I didn't need a law degree to recognize the look of guilt and shame on his face as he preceded the woman inside. So this was the woman he was cheating on my daughter with. Part of me wanted to march over there and confront him. But this wasn't my relationship to deal with. I had enough problems on my plate.

CHAPTER NINETEEN

The next morning, I walked back into court with my team at my heels. Outwardly, I was calm, measured, everything a client wanted in a lawyer. Inside? My stomach jittered like a bad neon sign, buzzing and flickering and about to go out.

I'd built this case brick by brick, and I knew we had it. The law was on our side. The facts were clean. Victory was already breathing down my neck.

And yet… winning what? The case, yes. But what was I about to lose?

As we passed through the marble, echo chamber of the courthouse, one of the admins caught me in the hallway. A smile, small talk about the weather, the kind of meaningless filler that kept the world turning was not on my docket today. I turned my face away to avoid being brought into any frivolous chatter and almost missed the bomb she dropped in the middle of the water cooler talk.

"Judge Bellamy's decided to retire. Permanently."

"Retire? He's been dangling that carrot for years."

The admin leaned closer, conspiratorial. "They've already asked Judge Marsden to take the role permanently."

Just like that, my lungs forgot how to work. Theo. Judge Marsden. Permanent.

I managed to keep moving, but inside I was collapsing. If Theo stayed on the bench, there was no us. Not unless I quit the only thing that still gave me purpose.

Law was my marrow, my spine. Without it, I'd just be another tired woman with too much regret and not enough fight left in her. No. I couldn't give that up. Which meant I had my answer, whether I liked it or not.

In the courtroom, Archie strutted like a rooster in a bespoke suit, puffed up for his client's sake. I knew the swagger for what it was: false bravado. Especially given the obscene hourly rate he was charging.

I glanced at my own client. Claire kept sneaking

looks at the former CEO, the man who'd treated her like she was disposable. I shifted my chair, deliberately blocking her view. She startled, looking up at me.

"It's going to be okay," I said.

Claire inhaled, shaky at first, then stronger. Nodded. She trusted me. God help her. But I trusted myself. In matters of the law at least. Matters of the heart, I seemed to lose every case.

"All rise," the bailiff barked.

Theo entered, solemn in his robes, every inch the judge. No trace of the man who smelled like soy sauce and salt. No hint of the man who had kissed me like the world was ending. His expression was carved from stone, his pace measured, deliberate, every step pulling the tension tighter.

He sat. Shuffled his papers with agonizing precision. The room held its breath.

"Please be seated," he said, voice calm and even.

Chairs scraped, murmurs died. The world narrowed to his mouth, the next words that would leave it.

"This case has presented questions of contractual obligation, corporate governance, and fiduciary responsibility. Both sides have argued vigorously. Counsel for the plaintiff"—his eyes flicked briefly,

briefly, toward me—"has laid out a narrative centered on breach of trust and material misrepresentation. Counsel for the defense has sought to frame this as a matter of risk, unfortunate but inherent in business dealings."

Theo's words were measured, surgical. No trace of bias, no hint of the man who'd once pressed me against a hotel door and left me breathless.

"The evidence submitted included board meeting transcripts, financial records, and testimony from both current and former employees. The credibility of the witness was weighed carefully, as was the consistency of the documentary evidence."

Claire trembled beside me. I kept my eyes fixed on Theo, willing myself not to betray anything. The case was iron-tight. Neat and tidy. There was no way I could lose.

"In reviewing the evidence, the court cannot ignore the pattern of omissions and the repeated failure to disclose material information to shareholders. The defense has argued that these omissions were immaterial, or at worst, unintentional. However, the testimony corroborated by internal emails undermines that assertion."

Archie shifted in his seat, his practiced smirk thinning.

Theo paused to turn a page. Deliberate. Controlled. Taking his time. I wanted to throttle him.

"The plaintiff's counsel has established to the satisfaction of this court that the omissions in question materially affected the decisions of investors and, by extension, the financial well-being of the plaintiff. The defense has failed to adequately rebut this."

My breath caught, but I forced myself to remain stone-faced. Nothing was won until it was said aloud.

"Having weighed the evidence presented, the court finds in favor of the plaintiff."

The words landed like a gavel to the chest. My client let out a sob. Her hand clutched mine as if I'd pulled her from a burning building. Relief poured off her in waves.

I gave her hand a squeeze. "It's over. You're okay."

Across the room, Theo was already moving on, instructing the clerk, voice smooth and impersonal.

I'd won. And I'd never felt more like I'd lost.

The courtroom cleared in slow waves. People shuffled out. Reporters whispered to each other. Archie huffed like a man cheated of his spotlight.

I took my time, stacking files, sliding papers into

my briefcase. Anything to delay the crash of adrenaline. Anything to delay being alone with the echo of my own thoughts.

"We're heading out to celebrate," said Amira. "You coming?"

I shook my head. "No. I just want a long bath and ten hours of unconsciousness. In that order."

Amira exchanged a look with Jackson—half concern, half amusement—and left me to it. Their footsteps faded, and for the first time in days, my world was silent.

"Ms. Russo."

The bailiff's voice cracked through the emptiness. I nearly dropped my briefcase.

"The judge asked to see you. In chambers."

I swallowed, throat dry. I rose on unsteady feet. My shoes suddenly weighed ten pounds each, but I carried them—and myself—toward the heavy door.

Inside, Theo was unfastening his robe. The black fabric slid from his shoulders, leaving him in shirtsleeves that stretched over muscle I had no business noticing but couldn't stop staring at. Broad chest, trim waist. A body that said discipline, not vanity.

I'd told myself I only wanted to win the case. That seeing him again was a complication I didn't need. But watching him hang his robe on a hook, I knew better.

I wanted this.

I wanted him.

The robe swung on the hook, empty and lifeless, while he turned toward me. His eyes found mine, steady and hot in a way no courtroom could contain. He wanted me too. I felt it like a hand pressed against my skin.

Before I could stop myself, I blurted out, "I know you were offered the judgeship."

Theo nodded once.

"If we disclose—if we're upfront now—they won't put us on the same case again." My voice was steadier than I felt. Inside, everything pitched like a ship in a storm.

The corner of his mouth lifted, slow and sad. "We don't have to do that."

I heard the thunk of the gavel in my mind. Rejection. My stomach dropped, throat tight. I swallowed hard, ready to armor myself, ready to walk out.

"I declined their offer."

It took a moment for the sense of those words to land. Declined. Offer. Put together, did that mean he wasn't staying on the bench?

I barely had time to breathe before his mouth

was on mine. The restraint we'd shown over the past few days combusted into something feral. His hands in my hair, my back slamming against the chamber door, mouths colliding like it had all been inevitable.

The last thought I had before thought ceased altogether was this: Being pressed against the door of a judge's chambers felt even better than the hotel room ever had.

CHAPTER TWENTY

Theo slammed me against the door like a verdict delivered—final and inescapable. And then his mouth was on mine. No deliberation, no jury instructions, no time for objections. Just a ruling handed down straight from his lips to mine.

The kiss was fire and salt and hunger, all the things I hadn't let myself admit I wanted. I should've pushed him away. I should've been the one dictating terms, cross-examining his every move, weighing the evidence. That's what I always did in relationships—controlled the record, set the precedent, made sure no man could walk away without me still holding the upper hand.

Theo didn't give me time to lawyer my way out.

He lifted me like I was nothing. My legs wrapped around his waist, automatic, instinctive, as if my body had skipped the opening arguments and gone straight to closing statements: *I want him.*

For half a second, my mind sputtered like a rookie associate flipping through case law for a precedent that didn't exist. *I'm too heavy for this. He'll drop me. He'll strain. He'll crack under the weight.*

Theo didn't falter. His grip was steady, his body solid. He carried me as if he'd been built for it. As if holding me wasn't a burden but his right, his privilege, his sworn duty.

His hand caught my wrists and tugged them above my head. One strong arm pinned me there, my body stretched against the hard plane of the door. He caged me without cruelty, held me without hesitation. I realized with a rush that stole the breath from my lungs that he could bear all of me: my weight, my fight, my anger, my need. And maybe more. Maybe the parts of me I never handed over to anyone.

My heart should have panicked. Should have objected, moved for dismissal, anything to get this thrown out before it became dangerous. Instead, it surged forward, reckless and eager, like it had already entered a guilty plea. My chest thudded against his, my pulse syncing with his like we were already bound by some silent verdict I hadn't agreed to argue.

It wasn't my heart that resisted. It was my brain. The strategist. The fixer. The one scribbling counterarguments on the back of cocktail napkins at three in the morning.

You're too old. He's too young. He's a judge. You're a lawyer. This is a conflict of interest, a mistrial waiting to happen. He's fire. You're tired. Walk away before you burn.

Every time I tried to rally a line of reasoning, Theo dismantled it with his mouth. His lips pressed harder, deeper, until my objections dissolved like weak evidence under cross-examination. My knees would've buckled if they weren't locked around his waist. My hands would've clawed at him if he hadn't caught them and held them high, reminding me in that devastatingly calm, confident way: *I've got you. You don't have to fight this.*

That was the most damning part. Not that he kissed me like a man starved. Not that he carried me like I was lighter than air. That he held me like he believed I could let go. That if I stopped bracing, stopped gripping control like it was oxygen, the world wouldn't collapse. He wouldn't collapse.

For someone like me, who had spent her entire life patching leaks and propping up beams no one else bothered to notice, that was more dangerous than any kiss. Because it felt like the truth.

And God help me, I wanted to believe it.

The door was cool at my back, his body scorching at my front, and I was caught in between like evidence trapped between prosecution and defense. No way out. No desire for escape. His tongue swept against mine, demanding, coaxing, a cross-examination I couldn't win and didn't want to.

Vaguely, I heard the zip of pants. Distantly, I heard the tear of a condom wrapper. Intimately, I felt him thrust into me.

Every nerve ending lit up like it had been dormant, benched for decades, waiting for this exact trial to come along. My skin tingled where his warm fingers gripped my wrists. My thighs clenched around the firm strength of him, every shift of his body a reminder that I wasn't too heavy, too much, too complicated. He could carry me. He wanted to.

My brain screamed mistrial. Conflict. Improper conduct.

My body overruled.

Motion denied.

My cry when I orgasmed was the verdict.

I could almost laugh at the irony: I'd spent my career fighting for justice, for truth, for the clean win. And here I was, surrendering with no defense, no appeal, no jury needed. The precedent was already written in the way my lips clung to his, the way my heart leapt toward him like it had been waiting for this judgment all along.

Theo deepened the kiss, his breath hot against mine, his hands iron and silk at once as he reached his own climax. And for once in my life, I didn't file a single objection.

I just let him win.

His mouth left mine for a heartbeat, just long enough for oxygen—and panic—to come rushing back.

My brain, that traitorous clerk who never knew when to shut up, immediately seized the gavel. Theo had said he turned down the bench here in Stillwater. That's what freed me, wasn't it? That's what made this possible.

If he wasn't taking the seat, what then? Did that mean he was just... walking away from the robe? From the steady paycheck, the title, the security?

Was he planning on being unemployed? Was this gorgeous, infuriating man expecting me to be his safety net? Because if I'd wanted to spend my fifties supporting a man-child, I could've stayed married.

I stiffened in his arms, the flare of panic sharp enough that he noticed.

"Did I hurt you?" His voice was gravel laced with concern. Still holding me as if I weighed nothing, still within kissing distance from my mouth.

I made myself meet his eyes. "If you're not taking the bench here, what exactly are you going to do?"

Theo's mouth curved, faint amusement tugging at his lips. "I'm not taking this bench. But Brookhaven's been courting me for months. They've offered me the seat. I told them yes. Now I can have my cake and eat you too."

His grin widened. Wolfish. Sure of himself in a way that rattled me.

God help me, I grinned back. Couldn't stop it, not with him standing there looking at me like I was both the ruling and the reward.

"So does that mean…" I hesitated, and then against all better judgment, I let the words tumble out. "Does that mean you're my boyfriend?"

The second the word left my mouth, I wanted to

die. Boyfriend. What was I, sixteen? Scrawling hearts in the margins of my Trig notes?

Theo grimaced.

My stomach bottomed out. I tried to scramble out of his arms and refile that last statement under "Stupid Mistakes Exhibits A through Z." I was too old for this. Too old for blushing, too old for labels that belonged to high school hallways and prom corsages.

"No. I'm not your boy anything, Lana. I'm your man."

The words landed like a ruling, overturning everything in my head. My chest seized. My breath hitched.

My man.

Not my burden. Not my project. Not another overgrown child to prop up while I crumbled. *My man. His woman.*

The humiliation melted, replaced by something hotter, heavier, terrifyingly close to hope.

I didn't speak. I didn't trust myself to. Instead, I lunged back into the kiss, letting his mouth swallow the last scraps of embarrassment. Letting his hands remind me of the verdict he'd already rendered—that I could let go. That I didn't have to carry him. Or anyone. He would carry me.

He pressed me harder against the door, his body reclaiming mine with a force that stripped away hesitation. My hands slid from where he'd held them pinned, tangling in his hair, clutching like I was starved for the feel of him. Which, apparently, I was.

Theo's lips dragged down my throat, his teeth grazing sensitive skin, his breath hot enough to scald. My head fell back against the wood, a sound escaping me that I'd long forgotten I was capable of making. Want. Pure, unfiltered want.

Some distant, responsible corner of my brain murmured about propriety, about decorum, about how this was a judge's chambers, not a hotel room. But the rest of me—the part that had been dry and starved and aching for far too long—silenced the objection.

He made quick work of my blouse, his fingers practiced, reverent, and hungry all at once. Each button undone felt like another defense stripped away, another piece of armor I didn't need with him. When his hands finally slid beneath the fabric, warm against bare skin, I shuddered.

"You're beautiful," he murmured against my collarbone, and the words nearly undid me more than the kiss. Not because I hadn't heard them before—I had, plenty—but because this time I believed them.

There was no more talking. Only sensation. His hands tracing, exploring, worshipping. My body arching, answering. The heat of him, the strength of him, filling the space until I couldn't remember why I'd ever thought this was wrong.

CHAPTER TWENTY-ONE

I was floating when I left the courthouse. No—higher than floating. Cloud nine, cloud ten, whichever cloud lawyers aren't supposed to touch because it interferes with objectivity. Theo and I had practically set the record for "quickest collapse of judicial decorum" in Stillwater Springs history. And I didn't care. For once, I didn't feel like the fixer, the nag, the mother, the ex-wife, the perpetual goddamn responsible adult. I felt… wanted.

But of course I'd insisted we leave separately. Call it self-preservation. Call it cowardice. I wasn't ready to broadcast anything. The verdict was still warm. The courthouse rumor mill hadn't even finished chewing its breakfast. And me? I wanted to remember how to be half of a couple before everyone else tried to write our closing arguments for us. In the relationship department, to call me rusty didn't begin to cover it. I was practically corroded.

And then there was the age thing. Ten years... or so. I wasn't sure. I should probably ask him that. Though did the age thing truly matter anymore? When he met me more than halfway. When he added nothing but a sense of lightness to my full plate. When he made me want to be my best self to match him.

The drive home gave me too much time to think. Stillwater Springs had always been beautiful in that suffocating way—postcard lake, gossip-clogged streets. I passed by Mr. Denton hosing down his driveway, knowing damn well he'd stepped out on his wife three times but always strutted into church like he was Saint Peter himself. I waved at Mrs. Collins, who ran the town bake sale with the zeal of a dictator while carrying on with her brother-in-law. Every corner of this town was crawling with dirty secrets—many of which I'd settled quietly outside of court, ones I'd overheard in whispers, ones I'd tucked away because people here loved two things more than pie: judging and pretending they had no right to judge.

And me? I'd been judged for years. For Myles cheating on me during our marriage. For Myles sleeping with girls young enough to borrow Brittany's prom dress after the divorce. For staying too long, for not leaving sooner. For holding it all together when everyone else was falling apart. And now I knew they'd be sharpening their knives for this—me and Theo. Not because of ethics. Not because of impropriety. But because of the one thing they'd never forgive: a woman my age daring to want more. To want him.

I crept into my house like a teenager trying to dodge a curfew, then stopped dead halfway to the kitchen. What the hell was I sneaking around for? Nobody in this place noticed me unless they needed something. I could probably have walked in naked with Theo slung over my shoulder and gotten less than a grunt from my family members.

I took two more steps inside, not bothering to try and muffle the sound of my heels on the hardwood, and nearly broke my ankle on a pile of luggage. My middle daughter's. Again. The girl collected souvenirs the way most people collected dust, and all of them lived in my living room.

I swore under my breath. I couldn't even navigate my own damn house without tripping over someone else's baggage—literal or otherwise. I never invited friends over anymore. Why bother? It looked like a hoarder's nest in here, and ninety percent of the junk wasn't even mine.

The kitchen was worse. Plates stacked like a Jenga tower in the sink, crumbs on the counter, a smell that suggested something in the fridge had given up weeks ago. Myles had stopped cleaning after the divorce papers were signed. The girls had never taken to chores. I didn't clean much myself— takeout had become my love language—but I paid for a maid service.

Around here, the unspoken rule was simple: if Mom didn't do it, Mom would pay someone else to do it. Either way, problem solved. Not their responsibility.

A thump from the basement cut through my self-pity. Myles. The eternal houseguest who refused to vacate. The man had wormed into my foundation like mold: persistent, ugly, impossible to fully eradicate.

I snapped. This was one adult I was going to hold accountable.

I stormed down the stairs and flung open the

basement door, ready to unleash years of pent-up rage. And then I froze.

Myles was in bed. With a woman I recognized instantly. Marcy, the pregnant woman I'd passed at Town Hall the other day. My brain short-circuited. Then it caught fire.

"Are you serious!"

Marcy sat up, eyes wide, hair wild. "Please don't tell," she blurted, as if I were her mother and not the ex-wife of the man currently sprawled beneath her. "It's just one last fling before I become a mom. One last ride before… responsibilities."

My blood pressure spiked so fast I heard ringing in my ears. "Get. Out."

Marcy scrambled for her clothes, tugging her shirt over her swollen belly. "Please don't tell my husband," she begged, voice trembling.

"You better hope that baby isn't his," I shot back, jerking a thumb at Myles.

"Ew." Marcy's nose wrinkled in disgust. "Like I'd get pregnant by someone who can't even take care of me."

She fled, leaving me with the man I'd wasted half my adult life on.

Myles climbed out of bed, penis still erect. He had always loved drama. His face was red with anger, not shame. "You can't just barge in here without knocking. This is my privacy."

"Your privacy?" My laugh came out sharp and jagged. "This is my house!"

The words rang hollow the moment I said them. Because it wasn't my house. It had never really been my house. Just a holding cell for everyone else's lives. Their mess, their noise, their endless needs. And me —the warden, the maid, the fixer-in-chief.

The fury drained out of me in one sudden, brutal wave. All that was left was the truth: I didn't want this life anymore. I didn't want to fight him. I didn't want to clean up after anyone. I wanted out.

I turned on my heels and left him shouting in the basement, his voice chasing me up the stairs. I didn't even bother to slam the door. He could rot down there for all I cared.

For the first time in years, I realized I wanted a different verdict for myself.

CHAPTER TWENTY-TWO

Theo opened the hotel room door looking like sin had gotten itself a good night's sleep. Bare chest, pajama bottoms slung low, hair sticking up in about twelve directions. Rumpled, delicious, and annoyingly unselfconscious about it. He blinked at me, rubbing the sleep from his eyes, and smiled like he'd been expecting me all along. He didn't ask what I was doing there. He just reached for me.

"I just ran away from home."

His arms tightened around me, firm, grounding, and then he tugged me inside. No interrogation, no raised eyebrows, no sharp remarks. Just… arms. Strong ones.

He sat me on the bed, tugged my shoes off, and

fluffed the pillows behind me like I was some honored guest instead of a half-broken woman who couldn't keep her own house from swallowing her alive.

Then, once I was wrapped up in his arms and his unwavering competence, he said softly, "Explain."

So I did. Hesitantly. Choking on the words half the time, like if I fed him too much of my mess he'd spit me out. Theo had given me nothing but peace and pleasure, and here I was dumping the landfill on his clean sheets. My family treating me like the eternal safety net. My house full of their junk, their chaos, their noise. Me, suffocating under it, drowning in it, unable to find a square foot that was just mine.

"Then I left," I said, voice thinner than I liked.

"And you came to me."

"You gave me space to breathe, space to remember who I was. When I went back home today… I saw it. How small it was making me. I couldn't do it anymore."

Theo rubbed slow, steady circles into the back of my neck with his thumb. Like he could untangle the knots I'd been collecting for the last twenty years one by one.

"You don't have to go back there. You can stay here as long as you like."

I balked, heat rushing to my face. "I'm not trying to move in with you."

"That's too bad. It would've made me making moves on you easier."

"You can't be serious." But God help me, I wanted him to be. I wanted someone to make it that simple.

"I'm always serious with you."

That stopped me cold. My brain scrabbled for some cross-examination, some way to poke holes in his testimony, because my heart was already leaning over the jury box, nodding along.

"Why?" I asked, sharper than I meant. "Why me?"

He didn't hesitate. "You're the full package. Brains and beauty."

"I have cellulite," I said, pointing to the soft patch of my inner thigh like it was Exhibit A.

Theo's eyes darkened, not with pity but hunger. My skin lit up under the weight of it. "I like the taste of it."

"You are a strange young man."

His grin flashed quick. Then his head dipped. Before I could launch another sarcastic objection, Theo's mouth brushed the inside of my thigh. He nipped lightly at the spot I'd just condemned, and I gasped like a woman half my age.

"You're a delicious woman who keeps me on my toes," he murmured against my skin.

My breath hitched. My brain tried to hang on to the familiar panic, the strategies, the counterarguments. But then he tilted his head, those eyes catching mine like a cross-exam I couldn't wiggle out of.

"I was hard every day of the trial. Listening to you construct your argument. The way your mind works? Lana, it turns me on more than anything else."

My heart was all in. Had been for a while, probably, though I hadn't wanted to see it. My brain was still pacing the floor, muttering objections, but it was losing ground fast. I gave up the argument for the night and once again let him win.

I let him pull off my clothes. I let him slip inside of me. I let him rock us both to one and then another orgasm. When he was done with that, I let him hold me and fell fast asleep.

THE NEXT TIME I opened my eyes, it was to morning light filtering through the hotel curtains. I slipped out of bed, pulled on yesterday's clothes, and padded to the door. My only plan was coffee: hot, black, and strong enough to qualify as a controlled substance.

I cracked the door open, and the universe decided to have a laugh at my expense. Because the door directly across the hall opened too. The man coming out of the other door was familiar. Because my brain was still fighting the losing battle of falling for Theo, it took a second for me to recognize Richard Lyle, the former CEO of Jennings Dynamics. The man whose defense I'd crushed the other day.

We both froze, like a bad courtroom sketch suddenly brought to life. His eyes widened. Mine narrowed. A whole silent deposition passed between us in three seconds: shock, guilt, and the dawning awareness that neither of us wanted to be standing there in front of the other.

Then she appeared. Claire. My star witness. Hair mussed, blouse buttoned wrong, face flushed in ways that had nothing to do with sleep.

I blinked once. Twice. Then the pieces slammed together so hard I swear I heard the gavel drop. They'd been sleeping together. The CEO and his own damn accuser.

My brain started running contingencies like a

panicked clerk rifling through case law. Mistrial? No, too late for that. Once the verdict's in and the gavel falls, mistrial's off the table.

Appeal, then? That's where the real fun begins. Grounds: witness credibility compromised. Collusion. Undisclosed relationship. Every motion I could file stacked up in my mind like dominos ready to tip.

But appeals don't come from judges. And they sure as hell don't come from prosecution counsel basking in their win. The defense could push it, though. If they got wind of this little post-trial affair, they'd smell blood. And suddenly my victory wouldn't look so clean anymore.

Post-trial motions. New trial. Sanctions. Hell, the board could even get involved. I'd built my whole case brick by brick, argument by argument, and now here was Claire, blowing a hole through the wall with one badly buttoned blouse.

My fingers itched to cross-examine her right there in the hallway. *When did this start? Before trial? During testimony? Did you perjure yourself? Were you sleeping with him while you swore to tell the truth?*

I wanted to throw questions like darts, watch them stick. But before I could open my mouth, arms slipped around my waist. Warm, solid, lips brushing the back of my neck like he owned me.

"Where are you going?" Theo murmured, voice rough with sleep.

And then he looked up and saw our audience: witnesses turned jury.

Theo went still behind me, every muscle locked. The kiss forgotten. The entire hallway became a courtroom. Four guilty parties, a vocal gossip mill down the hall ready to judge us all, and the suffocating weight of truth pressing down like the ceiling might crack.

Nobody spoke. Not me, not Theo, not the CEO or Claire. The silence itself felt like testimony. The case might be over, but the trial wasn't.

CHAPTER TWENTY-THREE

For one long second, the four of us—me, Theo behind me in his pajama pants, Richard, and Claire—just stood there like bad actors frozen in the world's most awkward courtroom drama.

I thought about dragging them into Theo's room to hash it out. But that hotel room still smelled like sex. I doubted theirs was any better. Neutral ground, then. Coffee in the hotel bar. At least caffeine couldn't be accused of impropriety.

We sat down at a little round bar table, four mugs of burnt hotel coffee steaming like a bad joke. Nobody spoke. The silence pressed thick. No one was ready to show their hands.

I let my gaze settle on Claire. She looked… small.

Tired. Her hair was damp, like she hadn't even bothered with a blow-dryer. Yesterday she'd been my warrior in a blazer, clear-eyed, firm-voiced, walking a courtroom through every corner of corporate rot. Now she looked like she'd traded her spine for a man's rumpled shirt.

I should've pulled her aside. Gotten her away from Richard before he sank his claws in. If I'd thought fast enough—if I'd been less shocked by seeing her shuffle out of his room like some walk-of-shame parody—I might have had a chance. Instead, here we were.

I leaned forward, ignoring Richard altogether, and reached across the table. My hand closed over hers. Her skin was clammy, fingers trembling.

"Claire," I said, low. "Are you okay? Do you want to leave with us?"

Her head jerked, startled. For half a breath I thought I'd nailed it, that she'd crumble, that she'd mouth *help me* like a hostage in a bad crime drama. But then she blinked twice, steadied, and said, "I'm fine. I'm exactly where I want to be."

I sat back, throat tight. Exactly where she wanted to be? No. No, that wasn't free will. That was indoctrination. That was trauma wearing fresh lipstick. Brainwashing, plain and simple.

I'd seen it before: clients stuck in abusive marriages, women convinced the cage was a sanctuary. The harder a friend or family member pulled, the tighter they clung to their abuser.

And now Claire, the woman who'd blown the whistle on corporate fraud and perjury, was sitting here holding hands with the very man she'd exposed —like a kidnap victim thanking her captor.

I wanted to shake her, drag her bodily out of that chair. Instead, I just clenched my coffee mug and prayed I wouldn't shatter it between my hands.

"It wasn't like that," Claire said, eyes darting to Richard. "When I worked for the company, Richard —he flirted, sure, but he never crossed a line. Last night was the first time."

Richard reached for her other hand like he thought this was a Hallmark special instead of a post-verdict debrief. "Everything's different now. I lost the case, the board tossed me out, and my wife walked."

Wife? That's right, he had a wife. She hadn't been at the courthouse. Hadn't sat behind him once during the trial. And now he was holding another woman's hands.

"Claire's the only one who stayed. She's the only one in my life that makes me want to be better."

Better. God save me from men who suddenly find redemption when their golden parachute doesn't open.

"Claire," I said, trying to keep my voice steady, "it's been one day since the verdict. One. And you think this is change? He's not Lazarus; he's just broke, humiliated, and horny."

Claire's eyes sharpened, and for the first time today, she looked like the witness I'd prepped for trial. "Says the woman sleeping with the judge."

I went rigid. Beside me, Theo leaned back, looking casual. But I knew him now. I knew when he was running the facts through his private chambers, weighing precedent, looking for the ruling that fit.

I wanted to object. To strike it from the record. But my mouth was dry, my brain stuttering.

Richard smirked, smelling weakness. "Don't get on your high horse, Counselor. Don't think I won't use this against you two if you try to interfere with me and Claire. You ruined my career. Try to take her from me and I'll ruin yours."

Claire's head snapped toward him, eyes wide, betrayal raw. "Richard—"

Theo sat forward then, calm as a man delivering instructions to a jury. "There's nothing to blackmail.

Lana and I disclosed our relationship prior to the case. The case is over. No impropriety to be found."

Theo looked straight at Richard, but his words were a sentence, not a suggestion. "If you've really changed, then prove it. Start over. Build something with Ms. Vesper if that's what you want. Maybe get divorced in the process. But don't drag her—or us—through more lies."

Silence stretched. The kind that hums in your teeth. Finally, Richard exhaled, a little ragged. He glanced down at the table, then at Claire. Claire slid her hand into his.

I should've screamed. Should've banged my fist like I was still in court. Instead I watched, jaw tight, as Claire rose, tugging him up with her.

"Thank you for everything you've done for me, Lana. I'm a big girl. I knew I was doing the right thing exposing corrup... the misdealings I found inside the company."

No, love, it was corruption. Not a misdealing, like the relationship she was clinging to. But Claire's eyes had that stubborn gleam I knew too well. The same one I'd carried when I swore Myles would finally grow up, when I told myself my girls would 'find their way' if I just held the world together long enough. Claire was choosing her poison. I knew better than anyone I couldn't wrestle a glass out of her hand if she was determined to drink.

"I feel like I'm doing the right thing now in giving Richard a chance to prove he's a changed man."

Richard's eyes flicked to their joined fingers like even he couldn't believe it. He blew out another breath, shaky like a fawn taking its first step. Then he steadied, like her faith had patched up his spine, like he was made stronger by her. Together, they turned and walked out.

I sat there with my cooling coffee and a knot in my throat. I hoped they made it. I hoped he proved himself worthy of her. I hoped she didn't spend her life fixing and smoothing and swallowing excuses for that broken man the way I had with my ex-husband.

A hand brushed mine under the table. Theo. Steady, warm, no agenda in the touch. He didn't squeeze like he was claiming me, didn't clutch like he might drown without me. Just… touched. Present.

"You're quiet," he said.

"Thinking."

"About them?"

"About me." I huffed out a laugh that sounded like it belonged to someone twenty years older. "Wondering if I've spent half my life trying to glue cracks in men who were bound to shatter, anyway."

"You know I don't need you to fix me, right? I don't need you to carry me, or save me, or smooth anything over." His thumb brushed the back of my hand, lazy, like he had all the time in the world. "I just want you. That's it. You. As you are."

Want. Not need. No conditions, no bargains, no ledger of debts to be repaid. Just… me.

It hit me then: I wasn't falling. I had fallen. Not the careful, calculated kind of falling where you tuck and roll. The reckless, bone-shattering kind where you don't care if you hit the ground because you wanted to jump in the first place.

CHAPTER TWENTY-FOUR

"I'm in love with him."

I dropped the words like I was announcing a terminal diagnosis, not some Lifetime Movie happy ending. Old Man Wendell snapped his newspaper open like the punctuation mark to my misery. Nosy bastard.

We were back at the coffee shop. Same cracked leather booths. Same chipped mugs. Same best friends who had been with me through my teenage crushes and failed marriage.

"With Theo?" Tessa leaned forward, completely unable to hide her I-told-you-so grin. "Why do you sound like that's a bad thing?"

"Because it is." I wrapped both hands around my

mug like it might steady me. "I'm going to ruin it. Like I ruin everything. My marriage. My kids."

"Oh, for God's sake," Celia said, rolling her eyes. "You have not ruined your kids. They're bright, smart, beautiful girls."

"Exhibit A," I said, ticking my finger on the table. "My youngest still can't land a job. Lives at home. Eats my groceries like she's carbo-loading for the Olympics."

"It's tough out there," Celia sniffed. "Zach's struggling in this job market too."

I ignored her. Exhibit B was burning a hole in my tongue. "My middle child? A vagabond. Flits around the globe, lands nowhere. You know what my house is? A glorified storage unit for all the crap she can't fit in her backpack."

Tessa shrugged. "Chloe's taking care of herself. Having experiences most people only dream about. That's not a failure, Lana, that's adventure."

"And finally, Exhibit C." I sat back, delivered it like a closing argument. "My eldest has terrible taste in men. Brittany's husband is cheating on her. History repeating itself."

Tessa didn't immediately disagree. She lifted her cup, sipped, then set it down. "Or—and hear me out —it's not about your kids at all. It's about you. For you, all I see is growth. In the past when you've dated men, you went for one-night stands. Men who didn't challenge you. Men who didn't entice you to stay. Theo does both."

"Theo's young," I said, the words tasting sour. "He'll get bored. He'll trade me in for a newer model before the warranty's even up."

But my girls weren't buying it. They heard the anxiety in my voice just like I did. Even Old Man Wendall heard it and gave me a sympathetic look.

Tessa shook her head, exasperated. "You're a catch, Lana Russo. You and Theodore have so much in common. Honestly, you and Myles? Complete opposites. Oil and water. I'm starting to think that whole 'opposites attract' trope is overrated. Even Celia and Bo are more similar than different. Me and Darnell? We worked because we were alike. Compatible. That's the stuff that lasts."

I stared into my coffee, black as tar, and tried to ignore the tiny, traitorous flicker of hope that maybe —just maybe—Tessa was right. Maybe I wasn't destined to ruin every good thing that landed in my lap. Maybe Theo wouldn't get bored, wouldn't trade me in for a shinier model with perkier everything. Maybe.

Movement in the window caught my eye. I

looked up, and there he was. Not Theo. My son-in-law.

Jack was ducking into a doorway across the street, practically glued to a woman's hip. He held the door for her, his hand brushing the small of her back in a way that had nothing to do with chivalry.

"Well, would you look at that," I said, sitting up straighter. "That's my son-in-law. And that's not my daughter."

Celia followed my line of sight, eyes narrowing like a hawk.

Tessa leaned forward, squinting, then huffed. "We don't know what he's doing. It could be innocent."

Celia and I both turned to her with the kind of pity reserved for children who still believed in Santa Claus. Unlike us, Tessa had never had her heart ripped out by betrayal. She didn't know the signs. The guilty body language. The secrecy. The way a man's hand lingered when it shouldn't.

Celia looked at me, one brow raised. "What do you want to do?"

I sat there for a beat, sipping my sludge, pretending to weigh the options. I could leave it alone. Pretend I hadn't seen. Let my daughter handle her own marriage. It wasn't my business. That's what a reasonable person would do.

But me? I'd never been reasonable. I was too old to start now.

I pushed back my chair. "Let's go confront the bastard."

Celia was on her feet in an instant, her eyes lighting up like Christmas morning. Tessa groaned but followed, muttering something about plausible deniability.

Together, the three of us marched out of the coffee shop, across the street, and into the building. I led the charge like a woman too damn tired to play polite anymore.

The three of us stopped in front of the door Jack had just disappeared through, huddling like teenagers about to sneak into a speakeasy. The building looked familiar, but I couldn't place its purpose.

"Wasn't this the old seamstress studio?" Celia squinted at the faded sign over the threshold.

"Could've sworn it used to be a pottery co-op," Tessa offered.

"Either way," I said, "Jack doesn't strike me as the macrame type."

I reached for the knob. Locked. Just as I stepped back, the door cracked open.

Out peered a woman who looked like she'd been

poured out of a martini shaker in 1965 and never bothered to sober up. Big cat-eye glasses that magnified her pupils to dinner plates, lipstick smeared half an inch outside her actual mouth, and a headscarf tied so tight her eyebrows were halfway up her forehead. Her gaze skated over us, sharp as a ruler in Catholic school.

She sniffed, eyes narrowing. "You're too young to come inside. Run along, little girls." And then she slammed the door.

The three of us stood there, blinking.

"Did she just call us too young?" Celia asked, her tone wobbling somewhere between affront and delight.

"I'm not sure whether to be insulted or complimented," said Tessa.

From behind the door came peals of laughter, whooping, the kind of cheering usually reserved for touchdown passes or Chippendales.

"Is there an orgy going on in there?" I wondered out loud.

Tessa turned pale and took a step back.

Celia's eyebrows shot up, and she rocked forward.

I banged on the door again.

It creaked open once more, and the martini

woman leaned out, looking smug. "Didn't I tell you girls to get lost?"

"I'm a lawyer," I snapped, stepping forward. "An officer of the court. You'd do best to let me in."

Her grin widened. "I know my rights, sweetheart. You don't have jurisdiction here."

"That's my son in there." My voice cracked like a whip.

That wiped the smirk right off her face. She studied me for a beat, then sighed. "Darling, you probably don't want to see what he's got going on in here."

"Try me." I shoved past her before she could close the door.

One step in, and I froze.

"Oh, dear God." My hand flew to my mouth, but it was too late. The image was already seared into my brain.

CHAPTER TWENTY-FIVE

"Mom, how could you!"

That was the welcome I got the moment I stepped through the front door of my house. No hello, no coffee, no grandchild thrust into my arms like a peace offering. Just pure, unfiltered fury.

Brittany wasn't wrong. How could I? How could I sneak around, break into a building I had no business in, and burn my retinas with the sight of my son-in-law dressed in nothing but glitter and a tuft of fake fur, like a Liberace nightmare someone ordered off Wish? Some things once seen can never be unseen.

At least we knew one thing now: Jack wasn't cheating. Unless you counted adultery with a glue gun.

"I knew I shouldn't have said anything to you. I knew I shouldn't have confided in you." Brittany's eyes sparked as she jabbed a finger at me.

"Stop." My hand went up like I was swearing in a witness. "You should've confided in me. That's what mothers are for. But before me, you should've talked to your husband."

Jack shifted his weight, staring at the carpet like maybe it would open and swallow him whole. Maddie clung to his hip, her little fingers rubbing the glitter still stuck to his cheek. It shimmered in the light, traitorous proof of his side hustle.

"I wasn't cheating, Britt. I would never..." Jack's voice cracked, and for once, the boy looked like a man trying to own up to something instead of duck it. "I made a bad investment. Lost more money than I want to admit. I just... I didn't want you to know. So I tried to make up the difference."

"By stripping for grandmas?" I muttered because God help me, the image was permanent.

"I wasn't stripping. I was modeling. They paid well. They wanted glitter and fur and..." Jack gave a helpless shrug. "I figured my pride wasn't worth as much as keeping my family afloat."

I almost applauded him for the honesty. Almost.

Brittany's lip trembled, then she launched herself at him, wrapping her arms around his neck, Maddie squished between them like a glitter-coated cherry on top. Jack clutched them both, whispering his apologies. Brittany whispered back that she loved him, no matter what. Maddie glared at me from the middle of her parents like this was somehow my fault.

And there they were: one happy family, framed in my doorway like something out of a greeting card.

I bit back the truth sitting on my tongue. That secrets had a way of rotting marriages from the inside. That lying by omission is still lying. But I stayed quiet.

For once in my life, I didn't fix, didn't argue, didn't point out all the cracks. They'd figure it out. Or they wouldn't. Either way, it wasn't my load to carry.

Myles, never one to let a tender moment breathe, cleared his throat. "Well, that's one way to humiliate yourself for a paycheck."

His tone had the same oily satisfaction it always did when he got to play patriarch. I half-expected him to puff out his chest like a pigeon.

I opened my mouth, ready to eviscerate him, but Brittany beat me to it.

"Dad, stay out of it. At least my husband is providing for his family and keeping it in his pants." Then she winced. "I mean—he's not letting anyone touch what's in his pants."

If shame could be bottled, I could've made a fortune off the secondhand embarrassment choking the air. Myles stared at his daughter like she'd just punched him in the gut. The girls might argue with him, but they never brought up his failings.

Out of the corner of my eye, I caught Emily leaning against the fridge, shoulders shaking with laughter she was trying to smother. Her phone was tilted just so, Chloe's face on the screen, pixelated but unmistakable. Of course. Why should only half of my children get front-row seats to this circus when modern technology could beam it straight across the world?

"Christ," Myles muttered, pinching the bridge of his nose like he was the victim in all this. "I'm going to bed."

Not so fast. "Actually," I said, cutting through the noise before he could slink off. "Since everyone's here, I have an announcement."

Every head swiveled in my direction, and for once, I didn't shrink under the weight of it.

"I'm seeing someone." I let that piece of evidence

drop into the center of the room. "It's serious. You'll meet him one day soon. But not here. Because I'm selling this house."

There it was. The real verdict. My heart gave a little lurch, but my voice stayed steady as I took in their stunned faces.

"I don't want to live here anymore."

The silence cracked all at once into chaos. Protests. Gasps. Brittany sputtered something about family legacy. Myles demanded to know where he was supposed to go. Emily was half-pleading and half-calculating about what she'd do next. Even Chloe's voice crackled through the phone, tinny but outraged, as though her storage unit of a bedroom had given her squatters' rights.

I held up my hand. It took a minute for the room to collapse into quiet again. "Ninety days. That's what you get. Take your things, find somewhere else, or buy me out. I'll sell this place for what's left on the mortgage. But one way or another, I'm moving out. And moving on."

The words sat heavy in the room, but for the first time in years, I didn't feel the need to soften them, to fix, to mother everyone into comfort. My chest hurt a little—like stretching a muscle that had been clenched too long—but beneath the ache was something unfamiliar.

Freedom.

Motherhood can trick you. You might think the job has an expiration date—eighteen years, a high school diploma, maybe college if you're lucky. But it doesn't stop. It just changes shape. You keep teaching lessons, even when your children are grown and carrying children of their own. Tonight, I taught them this one: that standing up for yourself isn't selfish. It's survival.

I'd raised three girls to speak their minds, fight their battles, demand their worth. Now it was my turn to prove I'd learned that lesson. For once, I wasn't mothering them.

I was mothering me.

CHAPTER TWENTY-SIX

"So you ran away from home?" Tessa asked, plopping down a tray of mismatched mugs.

"Yup." I straightened a stack of notebooks on one of the low tables. "And it feels great."

Tonight the yoga studio had that curated calm people pay too much for: soft golden lamps, mats rolled tight in their cubbies, incense clinging faintly to the air. Out the open windows, the spring burbled over stones, a sound that could make you believe in peace. But for me, the calm wasn't in the lighting or the water or even the overpriced sage Celia had burned a few minutes ago. It was in this: friends, laughter, and the delicious absence of anyone expecting me to fix their life.

"Are you and Theo moving in together?" Celia asked, arranging pens in neat rows like she was hosting a standardized test instead of a writing group.

"Absolutely not." I pulled a corkscrew across the counter and started in on the wine. "I only lived on my own for two years after undergrad before I got drafted into marriage and motherhood. I figure I need at least a decade to detox before I let a man's socks take up drawer space again."

Tessa leaned her elbows on the counter, smirking. "So he's not your boyfriend?"

"No," I snorted, setting the cork free with a pop. "He's my man."

That earned a cheer from both of them. The sound echoed off the studio's high rafters and made the place feel less like a yoga sanctuary and more like a girls' locker room after a winning game.

Tessa lifted her cup of tea like a toast. "Well, he's really not that young. He's only—"

The door swung open, and the rest of the women trickled in, chatter rising, laughter spilling, the kind of noise that swallows up confessions and replaces them with community.

I sat back against the counter, letting the moment wash over me. It wasn't the gurgle of the spring outside or the dim lights or even the promise of wine that made me feel settled for the first time in years. It was this: friends who knew me, a man who wanted me, and a family that no longer dictated the borders of my life. Peace didn't come from stillness. For me, it came from finally drawing a line in the sand and standing on my own side of it.

Celia rang the little brass bell, the one Tessa swore cleared energy but mostly just startled people into silence. "Tonight's theme is the moment you knew it was love."

Pens scratched almost immediately. Heads bent. A few smiles, a few sighs. Everyone diving in like this was simple. I stared at my blank page. My pen hovered, tip pressed just enough to bleed ink into the paper.

The moment I knew I loved Theo? Easy. It wasn't fireworks, or a kiss that stole my breath, or anything fit for a greeting card. It was on that quiet night when he let me be still. No fixing, no managing, no invisible labor with my name stamped on it. He hadn't swooped in or taken charge. He just gave me space to set everything down. Let me rest. And in that silence, my heart—stubborn, tired thing— opened the door. I didn't even mean to. I'd just reached for him, snatched him straight to my chest.

He'd laughed, that low rumble that made me believe the world might not be so bad after all, and he came willingly.

That was it. My moment.

But I didn't write a word of it. I wasn't about to put that on paper, hand it over like evidence in discovery, let anyone poke holes in it or suggest cracks in my argument. I wasn't submitting my feelings for Theo for cross-examination.

Celia drifted through the room, dispensing encouragement. A hand on a shoulder here, a whispered "good" there. When she reached me, she stopped. Looked down. Saw my blank page. Her teeth caught her bottom lip, the way they always did when she was trying to decide between truth and kindness. The last time she picked truth, we didn't speak for years.

I saved her the trouble. I reached for her hand. "I'm not a romance writer."

Her eyebrow lifted, sharp as a gavel strike. Agreement without a word.

"I've been thinking about writing a nonfiction book. Self-help, but not the kind that makes women feel like they need crystals and a vision board. No offense, Tessie."

"Some taken," Tessa said, sitting beside me, not

lifting her gaze from her page as she scribbled on and on about love and, likely, loss.

"I'm thinking about writing something for women who are trying to balance career and family and somehow wind up carrying both on their backs. Maybe call it *The Fixer's Guide to Burning Out Gracefully*. Or *Mother, May I Stop Now?*"

That got a laugh. Not just from my girls, but from some of the other women close by.

Celia laughed, and God, I'd missed that sound. Missed her. We'd been so tangled together as girls—sleepovers, whispered secrets, sworn loyalties—and then life had pulled us apart, spun us into marriages and messes that left little room for friendship. But here she was, standing with me in this yoga studio with her little bell and her too-soft voice, and I knew I wasn't letting her go again. Never again. No boundaries needed between us.

"I like it," she said. "And I think you're the perfect person to tell that story."

She turned to move on, but I squeezed her hand before she could. "Thanks," I said quietly. "For having my back the other day."

"I'll always have your back." Celia's smile softened, all warmth, no performance. "Every time."

And just like that, the years between us folded up.

No grudge, no gap, just Celia and me—what we used to be, what we'd found our way back to. Of course, then she had to ruin it.

"Just make sure your next girls' night doesn't include your son-in-law's glittery junk." She gave my notebook a little tap.

I snorted so loudly the women at the next table looked up. "No promises."

CHAPTER TWENTY-SEVEN

I stood before the jury, the words flowing as clean and sharp as a blade. My opening statement was tight, polished, airtight. I could feel the weight of it landing in the room. Every pause deliberate, every gesture measured. I didn't just have the facts on my side; I had inevitability.

I turned, still mid-stride, and there he was. Theo. Standing in the gallery, two travel mugs in his hands, grin cocky as ever.

Looking at him, I faltered. Just for a beat. Then I reeled it back in, finishing the statement like the pro I was. I didn't give anyone—jury, judge, opposing counsel—the satisfaction of knowing a man could make me forget my place.

When the defense finally got their turn, I sat back, listened, and knew. They were good. But I was better. We were going to win.

I leaned toward Amira, her pen tapping nervously against her notebook. "This one's yours."

Amira's head whipped around, eyes wide. "Mine?"

"You're lead counsel now."

For a heartbeat, she looked like she might cry. Then her spine straightened, chin up, shoulders back. She puffed herself full of courage like I'd just breathed life into her lungs. Good. She was ready.

"I think that's enough for today, people." Judge Whitaker gathered up her documents and adjusted her readers. There was a streak of gray in her jet black hair and not a wrinkle on her face. I needed to get the name of her moisturizer.

"We'll recess until Tuesday morning at nine sharp. In the meantime, I suggest you all enjoy the Jubilee—eat a funnel cake, listen to some music, maybe even remember there's life outside this courtroom."

A few chuckles broke the tension. Judge Whitaker gave the gavel a decisive rap. I liked her. Whitaker carried herself like a woman who'd been through the fire and decided not to waste time on smoke. About my age, too. Another one still standing when the world kept trying to knock us flat.

The courtroom thinned out until it was just me and my favorite judge left.

"What are you doing here?"

"Clear docket back in Brookhaven. So I decided to come watch you."

"Pervert."

"Guilty." Theo smirked and handed me one of the mugs. "Brought you coffee."

I took it. Sipped. Then kissed him. No warning, no finesse, right there under the dull stare of Lady Justice carved in stone above us.

He pulled back, startled but smiling. "Did you just make us courtroom official?"

I shrugged, sipping again at the coffee. "We're about to be small-town official at the Jubilee."

"Are you asking me out on a public date, Counselor?"

"That depends on your performance tonight, Your Honor."

That grin of his widened, slow and lethal. "Can I stay over at your place?"

I'd signed the lease on my apartment a week after "running away from home," and I hadn't looked back. The house was still in limbo—repairs needed since no one had stepped up to the mortgage offer. Brittany and Jack were solid now; Chloe had plans to dump her junk at her grandmother's; Emily was moving in with friends. Myles—I didn't ask. Didn't care.

What mattered was this: I had my space. My peace. And Theo had a set of keys. But he always asked before he came over.

"Yes," I said, simple as that. No hedging, no bargaining. My man could stay over tonight.

"Good. Because next weekend, I want to take you out of town. My birthday present to myself." Theo leaned in, close enough for me to smell the coffee on his breath. "I plan to unwrap you."

"Your birthday is next week?"

"Yeah. It's supposed to be a big one, apparently."

I opened my mouth, ready to head him off before he could say it—God help me, I didn't need the number—but he barreled right through.

"The big four-oh."

I blinked. Once. Twice. My brain short-circuited. "You're turning forty next week?"

"Yup."

"You mean… all this time… you've been almost forty?"

Theo nodded, taking another easy sip of his coffee, as if he hadn't just detonated a bomb in my chest.

"I thought you were in your thirties."

"I am in my thirties. For a few more days."

I just stood there dumbfounded. The math refused to line up. I'd spent weeks wrapping my head around this so-called age gap. Ten, maybe fifteen years. Me, the older woman. Him, the younger man. I thought I was a walking cliché. And here he was, not even ten years younger than me. I'd been building a case against myself out of thin air.

I narrowed my eyes. "Aren't you going to ask how old I am?"

"Don't care, so long as you're over twenty-one." Then he reached out, plucking the cup from my hand. "You can finish this once we're back at your place and I've made sure you're sober."

The memory of the first time he'd made sure I was sober hit me low in the gut. Coffee before sex was our unspoken contract. I should've argued, should've rolled my eyes and told him he wasn't the boss of me. But instead I let him take it because I didn't have to be in charge.

And that felt like the real gift.

Want to read Celia's story?
Check out *Still Healing*
at JemJohnsonBooks.com

ABOUT THE AUTHOR

Jem Johnson writes small-town, big-heart romances about women over forty rediscovering desire, purpose, and the power of second chances. A firm believer that it's never too late to fall in love—or finally choose yourself—Jem crafts emotionally rich stories filled with family ties, lifelong friendships, and slow-burn chemistry that simmers through every season of life. When she's not writing, you'll find her people-watching in a coffee shop, filling her planner with too many stickers, or plotting her next fictional Jubilee. *Stillwater Springs* is her love letter to women who've done the work… and are ready to feel alive again.

Visit my web store for steals, deals, and access to my books before they're on retailers! https://jemjohnsonbooks.com/

ALSO BY JEM JOHNSON

STILLWATER SPRINGS
Still the One
Still Got It
Still Healing
Still Mine
Still Yours
Still Home